RUDOLF STEINER
AND ANTHROPOSOPHY
FOR BEGINNERS

LÍA TUMMER

ILLUSTRATED BY LATO

Clairview Books Ltd.,
Russet, Sandy Lane,
West Hoathly,
W. Sussex RH19 4QQ

www.clairviewbooks.com

Published by Clairview Books, UK, 2024

Previously published by Writers and Readers Publishing, Inc., New York, 2001

Translated by Patricia Pitchon

© Lía Tummer and Horacio Santana 2001

This book is copyright under the Berne Convention. All rights reserved. Apart from any fair dealing for the purpose of private study, research, criticism or review, no part of this publication may be reproduced, stored in a retrieval system, or transmitted in any form or by any means, electronic, electrical, chemical, mechanical, optical, photocopying, recording or otherwise, without the prior written permission of the copyright owner. Inquiries should be addressed to the Publishers

The rights of Lía Tummer and Horacio Santana to be identified as the authors of this work have been asserted by them in accordance with sections 77 and 78 of the Copyright, Designs and Patents Act, 1988

A CIP catalogue record for this book is available from the British Library

ISBN 978 1 912992 59 1

Cover by Morgan Creative featuring art by Lato
Printed and bound by Halstan & Co. Ltd., Amersham, Bucks.

Contents

Introduction	1
Born of the woods	**6**
Masters	18
Goethe	22
Nietzsche	36
Haeckel	37
Theosophy	50
Marie von Sivers	55
The birth of anthroposophy	**58**
The realms of nature	64
The image of man	66
The evolution of the individual	70
Reincarnation and karma	72
The human aura	76
The path of knowledge	79
The Akashic Record	85
Steiner's cosmology	88
The birth of human individuality	91
Anthroposophy and Christianity	96
2nd phase of Anthroposophy:	
the artistic impulse (1910-1916)	**99**
The 'drama mysteries'	100
The Goetheanum	103
Eurythmy	114
3rd phase of Anthroposophy:	
practical applications (1917-1925)	**121**
The threefold structuring of the Social Organism	123
The Waldorf schools	127
The Waldorf method	134
Therapeutic education	141
An anthroposophical approach to medicine	143
Bio-dynamic agriculture	155
The Community of Christians	156
The Goetheanum fire	159
1924 to 1925	161
Anthroposophical organisations	166
Bibliography	167
Index	168
The Authors	172

Introduction

1900... One hundred years ago, when Europe first began to live by electric light, to communicate via telephone and telegraph, to travel by car, electric tram, airplane, and to be dazzled by the 'magic' of cinema...

...when, exultant, Europe celebrated her technological achievements at the foot of the new tower...

World's Fair Paris (1889)

...and anxiously buried itself in the existential vacuum of 'the end of the century', reading Zola, Tolstoy, Shaw, Ibsen, and discussing the theories of Darwin, Haeckel, Marx...

Rudolf Steiner began to expound his very personal 'path of knowledge': anthroposophy.

The explosion of human creativity at the end of the nineteenth century represented the climax of the materialist concept of the universe, inaugurated by the 'scientific revolution' of the sixteenth and seventeenth centuries.

THE DISCOVERY AND THE USE OF SCIENTIFIC REASONING BY GALILEO IS ONE OF THE MOST IMPORTANT CONQUESTS IN HUMAN THOUGHT.

So radical was the revolution produced by **Galileo** in the history of culture, that his era is seen as the end of the Middle Ages and the beginning of the Modern Age—the 'day the universe changed'.

MIDDLE AGES 1600	MODERN AGE 1900
- The rule of dogma - Aristotelian logic - Religion - Ptolemy's cosmology (earth = the centre of the universe) - Man = the son of God - Contemplation - Devotion, faith	- The rule of reason - Cartesian logic (mechanistic) - Positive sciences - The cosmology of Copernicus, Kepler (the earth moves around the sun) - Man = the superior animal - Active life - Rationalism, materialism

The world, trained for centuries to completely separate science and religion, knowledge and faith, body and soul, matter and spirit, did not accept that integration.

In the seventeenth century Galileo had had to explain to humanity that there is an infinite universe beyond the firmament that, until then, was believed to be the limit of space. In the twentieth century Steiner tried to explain to humanity that there is also a reality beyond the 'firmament' that modern man sees as the limit of life.

Just as the Church felt threatened by the 'revolutionary' ideas of Galileo, fighting him in life, and 'ignoring' him for centuries, so the academic world has managed to virtually ignore Rudolf Steiner for the last hundred years.

One hundred years have passed…

...and effectively not only is Rudolf Steiner listened to with growing interest, but many of his proposals have been used to reform a number of areas of human endeavour: education, medicine, agriculture, architecture, art, religion, social organisation, etc. The success of diverse initiatives demonstrates that anthroposophy is not a mystical and abstract mental construction, but a cosmovision able to enrich human life, even in its most practical aspects.

Born of the woods

Towards the end of his life, although already ill, Rudolf Steiner began to write his autobiography:

Both my father and my mother were true children of the magnificent woods of Lower Austria, to the north of the Danube. My parents loved the land from which they came and when they spoke of their experiences there, one could see how their souls had never left that small country, despite destiny having led them to spend the greater part of their lives far from it.

Johann Steiner (1829-1910)

Franziska Blie (1834-1918)

As a young man, Rudolf Steiner's father had travelled through the woods of his native land as a hunter in the service of a Count. On meeting **Franziska Blie**...

Over the years—during which time a daughter and another son was added to the family—the Steiners were sent to different stations in the same Austro-Hungarian region.

The father's work formed part of the family's daily life.

Young 'Rudi' did not miss the arrival or departure of the few daily trains that brought different characters from the village and its surroundings, including the Count from the nearby castle, along with his entourage.

He was also captivated by his father's telegraphic duties which he learned to carry out as a child.

Since Johann's salary was modest, the children had to share the household chores and the work in the orchard.

The parents were always ready to spend the last of their savings for the good of their children.

"BUT THERE ARE HARDLY EVER ANY SAVINGS LEFT."

Rudolf Steiner grew up, therefore, in an austere atmosphere, surrounded by unspoiled nature, in small railway towns buried amidst the greenery of fields and woods, framed by the snowy peaks of the Alps on the horizon.

TODAY, AFTER BREAD WITH BUTTER OR CHEESE, WE'LL HAVE RASPBERRIES FOR DINNER!

On his walks through the woods he would collect strawberries, gooseberries or raspberries.

He also collected wood with the local inhabitants, simple and unpretentious people who were always cordial, always ready to chat.

People didn't even notice that the person who ran ahead of them was just a boy. In the depths of their souls they were still children, even when they were seventy years old.

The village school, where a schoolmaster taught five grades simultaneously, could not teach Rudolf much more than reading. However, thus armed, he eagerly went forth to conquer the world of knowledge. He began when he was just eight years old, when a geometry book fell into his hands:

I devoted myself to studying geometry. For weeks my soul was full of convergences and likenesses of triangles, rectangles and polygons.

WHERE DO PARALLEL LINES INTERSECT?

To be able to perceive something purely in the realm of spirit filled me with inner joy.

GEOMETRY GAVE ME A FEELING OF HAPPINESS FOR THE FIRST TIME.

I realised then that the knowledge of the world should be carried within, in the same way as geometry. For me what is spiritual, 'what is seen', was as real as 'what is unseen'.

When Rudolf Steiner was eleven, his father, who wanted a 'solid' future for his son, sent him to the secondary school in the nearest town.

There Rudolf felt intense affinity with the clear and logical structure of mathematics.

To be able to follow the rhythm of the classes and satisfy his passionate interest in all subjects, he had to devote his free time to making good the deficiencies with which his primary schooling had left him.

He began to give private lessons to his schoolmates, to help to pay for his studies.

It was the time of the first 'pocket book editions' and his earnings allowed him to purchase the works of the great philosophers. He studied them fervently.

Since the history classes at school did not live up to his desire for knowledge, Steiner re-bound his history book interweaving among its pages those of **Kant**'s *The Critique of Pure Reason* in order to be able to read, re-read and ponder it during history lessons.

His school, which was mainly technically oriented, did not teach Greek or Latin and so Steiner learned those languages on his own. He also began to prepare himself in all the subjects his private pupils needed to learn—including even accountancy.

13

In order that his son would be able to study at the Technical University in Vienna, Johann Steiner asked for a transfer to a place near the capital, although this was less convenient and agreeable for him. His son's exceptional aptitude for mathematics reaffirmed the father's wish that Rudolf should follow a technical career.

When he began his university studies in 1879, Rudolf Steiner registered for biology, chemistry, physics and mathematics. At the same time, he attended classes in philosophy and literature with the great teachers of the time. He never abandoned his intensive reading and research, especially into themes that caught his interest.

At that time he felt committed to seeking the truth through philosophy.

He would study mathematics and natural sciences, but to establish a link with these topics, he would base his results on a reliable philosophical foundation.

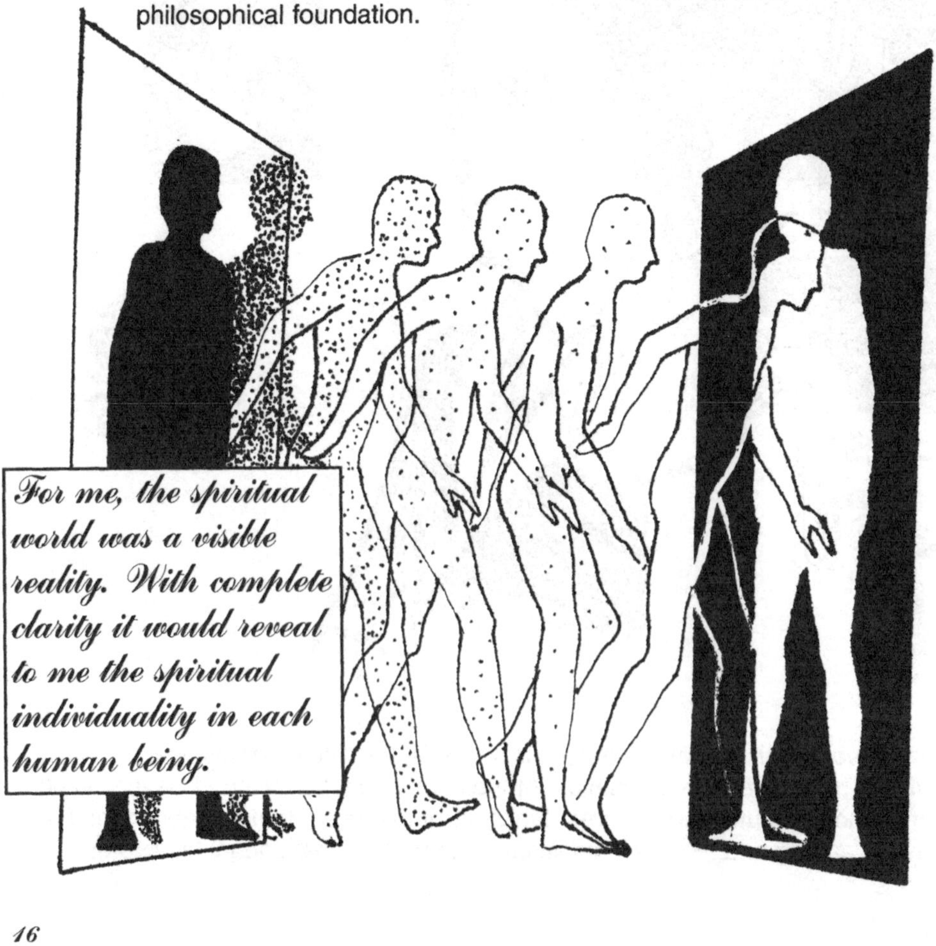

For me, the spiritual world was a visible reality. With complete clarity it would reveal to me the spiritual individuality in each human being.

According to what Rudolf Steiner related much later, he was seven years old when he saw the first tenuous manifestations of a world not perceived with the physical senses. At that time a relative—who he learned later had just committed suicide in a remote place—presented herself to him and begged him to protect her. The boy immediately understood that this was not a physical presence: it was no more than the first indication of a very exceptional clairvoyant ability that deepened more and more throughout his life.

From that first experience Steiner intuited that if he related what he perceived so clearly in his inner world, he could not count on the approval of his elders.

My father considered himself a 'freethinker'. He did not like me to go to church. He would have been even less willing to accept my inner experiences.

Rudolf was baptised in the village's Catholic church and had his first religious experiences as an acolyte.

He learned to keep silent. With great fortitude and equilibrium he began his solitary inner journey at an early age.

Masters

It was not until he was eighteen that Steiner met someone with whom he could share his inner experiences:

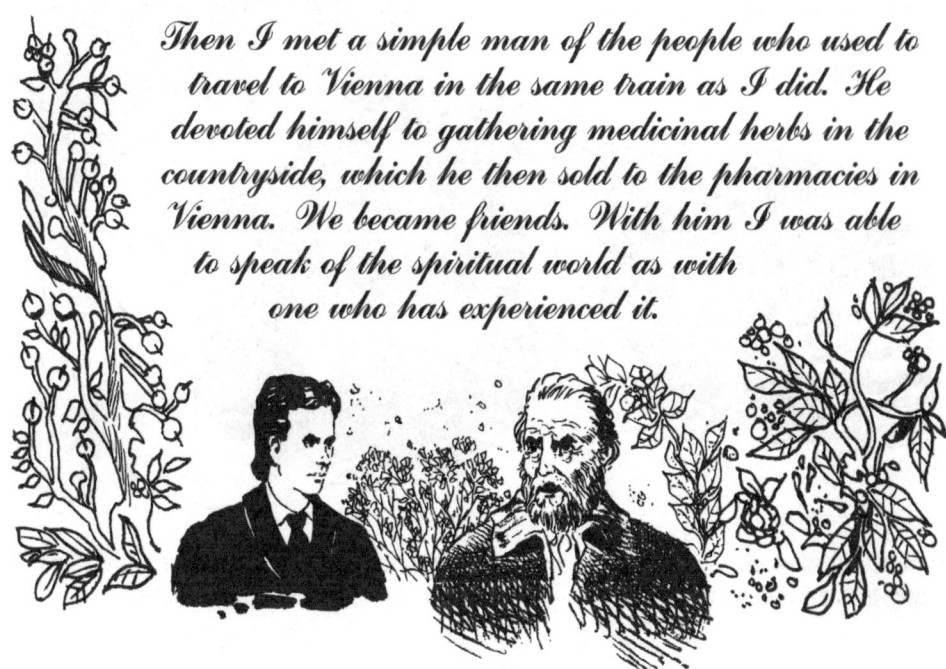

Then I met a simple man of the people who used to travel to Vienna in the same train as I did. He devoted himself to gathering medicinal herbs in the countryside, which he then sold to the pharmacies in Vienna. We became friends. With him I was able to speak of the spiritual world as with one who has experienced it.

He lacked education in the sense of formal schooling. He had read many mystical books, but what he said was not coloured at all by that reading. It emanated from an elemental and creative spiritual knowledge... Being with him, one could reach deeply into the secrets of nature.

And in this way I began to feel as if I were with a soul from very ancient times, who— unchanged by civilization, science and the concepts of the present— rought me closer to an instinctive knowledge from far-off times.

There was another person of transcendental significance for Steiner's evolution, whose name he also never mentioned.

Through the collector of herbs Steiner met a 'spiritual master' who—from the anonymity of a humble bourgeois existence—knew how to be a valid interlocutor for his inner experience and a guide when he forged his future work.

At that time the young Steiner had already set himself an ambitious and daring mission in life: to reunite science and religion, matter and spirit.

But how to achieve this? How to transform and overcome the unilateral stance of the modern natural sciences? How to tame the dragon of extreme materialism?

The dialogue with the 'master' strengthened his conviction that he would only be able to harmonise his own inner experiences of the spiritual world with the materialist concept of his surroundings when the intellectual consciousness of his time could become his own. Only if he mastered the forms of reasoning of the 'scientific method' and became fully aware of the limitations of the scientific concept of the universe could he speak to the spirit of his contemporaries.

Steiner then redoubled his efforts to acquire a comprehensive mastery of the most varied areas of scientific knowledge.

Goethe

Among the great academic figures who embodied university life in Vienna at that time—many of them vividly described by Steiner in his autobiography—was **Karl Julius Schröer**, professor of German literature, who won his affection and devotion. All Schröer's erudition and sensibility flowed together in his admiration for **Goethe**.

...Schröer lived so intensely in the being and work of Goethe that with each feeling or thought that arose in his soul, he would ask himself: would Goethe have felt or thought in the same way?

Karl J. Schröer (1825-1900)

Under Schröer's paternal tutoring, Steiner acquainted himself with the literary work of Goethe.

With the same intensity with which he approached all subjects, Steiner studied Goethe's work—including his lesser-known scientific investigations—until the poet's thought began to throw light on his own search.

As he delved into Goethe's writings on optics, botany and anatomy, his conviction grew that the purely materialist concept of the modern natural sciences was capable only of explaining dead nature, not life. In Goethe he found the possibility of describing the organic world and uniting matter and spirit.

Inspired by Goethe's thought, Steiner began to build a bridge between scientific knowledge and his own empirical observation of the action of spiritual forces.

Through the mediation of Professor Schröer, Steiner was entrusted with editing Goethe's scientific writings for a publication of the complete works of the writer, with a prologue by Schröer himself. At the age of 21, Steiner was by far the youngest contributor.

In one of the rooms on the top floor of the railway building that his parents occupied at the time in a little village in the mountains, Steiner wrote his commentaries on Goethe's scientific works.

In the midst of the great cultural effervescence in the Vienna of his student days, Steiner began to acquaint himself with various circles of well-known philosophers, theologians, writers, musicians and painters. He shared the feelings and thoughts of all those colourful individuals. with deep and affectionate interest.

It was easy for me to feel at home within other personalities, within other ways of thinking. In my own spiritual world, however, I could not receive visitors.

The paths of his inner experience led him along such steep slopes that no one managed to accompany him. He had to advance as a solitary traveller.

The obligatory meeting places of the intellectuals—artists, thinkers and politicians—of monarchical Vienna were the traditional cafés.

Steiner was such a frequent visitor to one of these, that for some time it was even used as his postal address. It was there he wrote his first book on Goethe's theory of knowledge.

While he researched more and more deeply into human knowledge and existence, Steiner continued to earn his living through individual tutoring. Once he had concluded his university training, he was employed—again through the recommendation of Professor Schröer—as a tutor to four brothers. One of the children, who was ten years old, suffered from hydrocephaly. When Steiner came into this family, with whom he lived for six years, the boy's disability was so great that he was considered ineducable. Developing, step by step, a method to reach him, Steiner managed in two years to improve the boy's health and mental development to such a degree, that he was able to enter secondary school and continue his studies normally until he eventually became a doctor and, as such, a victim of World War I.

This educative experience was of providential importance for Rudolf Steiner's future educational and therapeutic initiatives.

TRULY IT WAS THEN THAT I CONDUCTED MY STUDIES OF PHYSIOLOGY AND PSYCHOLOGY.

Once again a reference from Schröer brought the young expert in Goethe's scientific work to the attention of the authorities at the **Goethe and Schiller Archive** in Weimar, Germany.

HOW MUCH I OWE TO SCHRÖER!

In 1890, at the age of 29, Rudolf Steiner was called to the recently-created Archive to study and publish Goethe's still-unedited scientific writings. Steiner abandoned his native land, conserving from it throughout his life, its warm dialect and its affable and conciliatory manner. He moved to Weimar with feelings of nostalgia for the social and cultural exchanges he had enjoyed in Vienna, but also with an enormous sense of expectancy...

THE GREATEST GERMAN MASTERS HAVE PASSED THROUGH HERE!

29

When I stood for the first time before the magnificent double statue, I felt as if suddenly everything I had reflected on and thought about Schiller and Goethe acquired a new life...

Monument to Schiller and Goethe in front of the National Theatre.

From the eighteenth century onwards the city of Weimar, capital of the Great Duchy of Saxony-Weimar, became the cultural centre of Germany, even of Europe. It was the 'German Athens'.

The ducal family made great efforts to attract to Weimar artists and thinkers of the stature of **J.S. Bach**—who was an organist there from 1708 to 1714—and **Schiller**, **Herder**, **Wieland**, etc. Goethe was an intimate friend of the Great Duke Karl August and advisor in many affairs of state. In his autobiography, Steiner described his stay in the city of **Richard Strauss**, **Franz Liszt**, **Henrik Ibsen** and **Gustav Mahler**.

Steiner lived in Weimar for seven years, until he completed the work entrusted to him by the Archive. The annual report of the Goethe Society for 1897 described his work as Goethe's editor:

> *What Rudolf Steiner has achieved through the happy union of critical and productive abilities has deserved the praise of all men of knowledge. Thanks to his tireless and committed efforts, we now have available a batch of documents coherently ordered and presented, which assure a greater and fuller evaluation of Goethe as a naturalist.*

Very few people understood Steiner's deeper objective of promoting a cultural renewal based on the Goethean concept of the world.

When Steiner came as a tenant to the house of **Anna Schultz**, the domestic miseries he had been suffering in Vienna and Weimar came to an end.

Anna—mother of four girls and one boy—offered him a home, attended selflessly to his needs and showed herself to be grateful for the support Steiner gave her in the education of her children.

Anna Schultz (1853-1911)

In fact I was not the only one who enjoyed the warm welcome I had found. When my friends, on occasion, wanted to feel comfort and privacy, they would come to see me in the family home. And I have reasons for supposing that they felt very well there.

Steiner eventually married Anna, although very soon the incompatibility of their respective aims in life distanced them. Nevertheless, not long before she died, Anna confided to one of her daughters:

THE TIME I SHARED WITH RUDOLF STEINER WAS THE MOST BEAUTIFUL OF MY LIFE!

Steiner's sociable character soon led him to a circle of writers, scientists, artists and philosophers in Weimar. He was well received. There he met the great personalities of his time.

EACH POINT OF VIEW HAS ITS REASON FOR EXISTING...

It was one of Rudolf Steiner's great maxims that he would not ever surrender himself to a cause or a personality, without having familiarised himself with the opposition.

This attitude was not a mere self-imposed 'exercise', but a profound dedication to steeping himself in foreign ideas.

Faced with different currents of thought, Steiner always practised a positive attitude which could set aside all the deviations and arrive at the 'seed of truth' of each of them. He not only rescued from each ideology that part which deserved to be developed, he also valued the historical function it was destined to fulfil within the evolution of humanity.

With that positive attitude, Steiner confronted, for example, the annotated edition of the complete works of **Schopenhauer**—whom he admired for his 'obtuse' genius, although his pessimistic philosophy was totally alien to him—and the German writers **Jean Paul, Wieland** and **Uhland**.

Arthur Schopenhauer
(1788-1860)

There are two German thinkers from his time that Steiner sought to vindicate with such special fervour that he was eventually considered a 'partisan' of these, despite the fact that they represent viewpoints very distant to his own: **Nietzsche** and **Haeckel**.

WHAT DOES STEINER'S SPIRITUAL GOETHEAN VIEW HAVE IN COMMON WITH THE NAÏVE MATERIALISM OF HAECKEL?

IF YOU COULD CHOOSE TO BE SOMEONE ELSE, WHO WOULD YOU LIKE TO BE?

FRIEDRICH NIETZSCHE BEFORE HE WENT MAD.

Nietzsche

During his time as a student in Vienna, Steiner began to read **Friedrich Nietzsche**; He soon recognised that the philosopher's search was both brilliant and tragic.

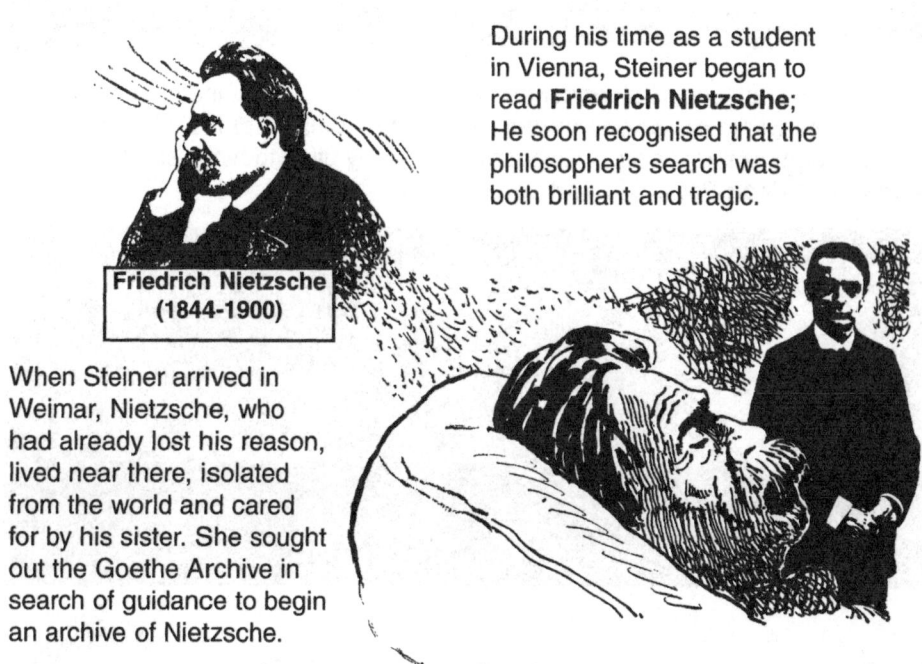

Friedrich Nietzsche (1844-1900)

When Steiner arrived in Weimar, Nietzsche, who had already lost his reason, lived near there, isolated from the world and cared for by his sister. She sought out the Goethe Archive in search of guidance to begin an archive of Nietzsche.

Steiner went to the Nietzsche home to offer his collaboration. He was one of the few visitors who managed to see the philosopher in his bed of shadows. Intimately moved by that 'absent presence' and by what the task of ordering the library of the fallen genius meant, Steiner wrote his book **Friedrich Nietzsche: Fighter for Freedom** (1895). After the philosopher's death he published two psychopathological works and held many comemmorations and conferences on Nietzsche's thought.

While revising Nietzsche's books, generously provided with vehement comments in the margins, Steiner read into his soul.

Haeckel

While Steiner worked in Weimar the violent attacks that **Ernst Haeckel** suffered as German spokesman for Darwin's theory of evolution from the Church and reactionary circles of the cultural milieu, were at their most virulent.

Steiner was convinced that the theory of the evolution of the species—promoted particularly by Darwin and Haeckel—should be incorporated into the consciousness of modern man, even if the early explanations should turn out to be primitive and not very convincing.

In his work **Haeckel and his Opponents** (1899) Steiner showed the strength of Haeckel's position and the weakness of the theologians in the face of the reality that natural sciences began to unveil about the evolution of nature and mankind.

Everything Steiner studied and reflected on during those years took shape in one of his fundamental works:

The first edition in 1894 carried the subtitle 'Results of the animic investigation according to the method of the natural sciences', a clear reference to Steiner's main objective: to apply the exactitude of observation of the modern natural sciences to external nature and also to the inner world.

Steiner had been practising meditation as a means to knowledge. With time, that practice became a need that was as vital as breathing.

The idea no longer has the value of knowledge, but rather in its permanent repetition it creates an inner life that leads to a deeper and deeper comprehension of the spiritual world.

It is not enough to know that a thought is truthful; it is necessary to have lived with it intimately for many years.

Upon completing his work in Weimar and soon after reaching the age of 35, a fundamental change of attitude began to take place in him.

Despite an intense cultural and social interaction with his milieu, and a fruitful intellectual production—by then he had published 95 works—until that time his main aim had been to enter more and more deeply into the spiritual world, growing 'inwardly'.

From then on he also began to grow outwardly, moulding his own destiny, giving to humanity his internal treasure.

The Rudolf Steiner has 'awoken' who can 'awaken' others.

From childhood Steiner had suffered a certain spiritual isolation, because what he perceived so clearly did not find resonance even in those who approached him with the most sincere affection and respect: he reached a point in conversations where he could no longer explain himself.

AND THE QUESTION AROSE: SHOULD ONE REMAIN SILENT?

Rudolf Steiner decided then to emerge from his silence and to begin to 'say everything it is possible to say'.

Humanity has sought a knowledge of the spiritual world throughout its entire history.

In antiquity that knowledge was conserved in the 'mysteries' or places of ritual worship which prepared the few elect for the transmission of 'occult knowledge'.

These 'initiates' were, then, the bearers of ancient knowledge, which specifically derived its strength from being 'esoteric'. (secret or hidden), in contrast to 'exoteric' knowledge, which is communicated openly.

If I wished to develop public activities in favour of spiritual knowledge, I had to decide to break with that tradition.

We live in a time when any new discoveries need to be promulgated. And the idea of keeping knowledge secret is an anachronism.

Also, I did not have a commitment to anyone to keep silent. Since I never accepted any 'ancient wisdom', everything I have learned in the area of spiritual knowledge is purely and exclusively the result of my own research.

Determined to speak, Steiner had to find a medium to express himself. Since he lacked economic resources and the necessary influence to found a publication himself, he acquired the **Magazin für Literatur**.

Transformed into an organ of the Free Literary Association, the magazine—based in Berlin—was a focus for the young generation of German writers.

The *Magazin fur Literatur* had barely enough subscribers to survive.

Steiner then moved to Berlin, to take up a regular position as a lecturer at the Free Literary Association: in order to maintain the magazine, he had to win over the Association's members as readers.

His aim of broadening his circle of readers also brought him close to the Drama Association, devoted to producing avant-garde plays which did not find acceptance or commercial success in the classical theatrical venues.

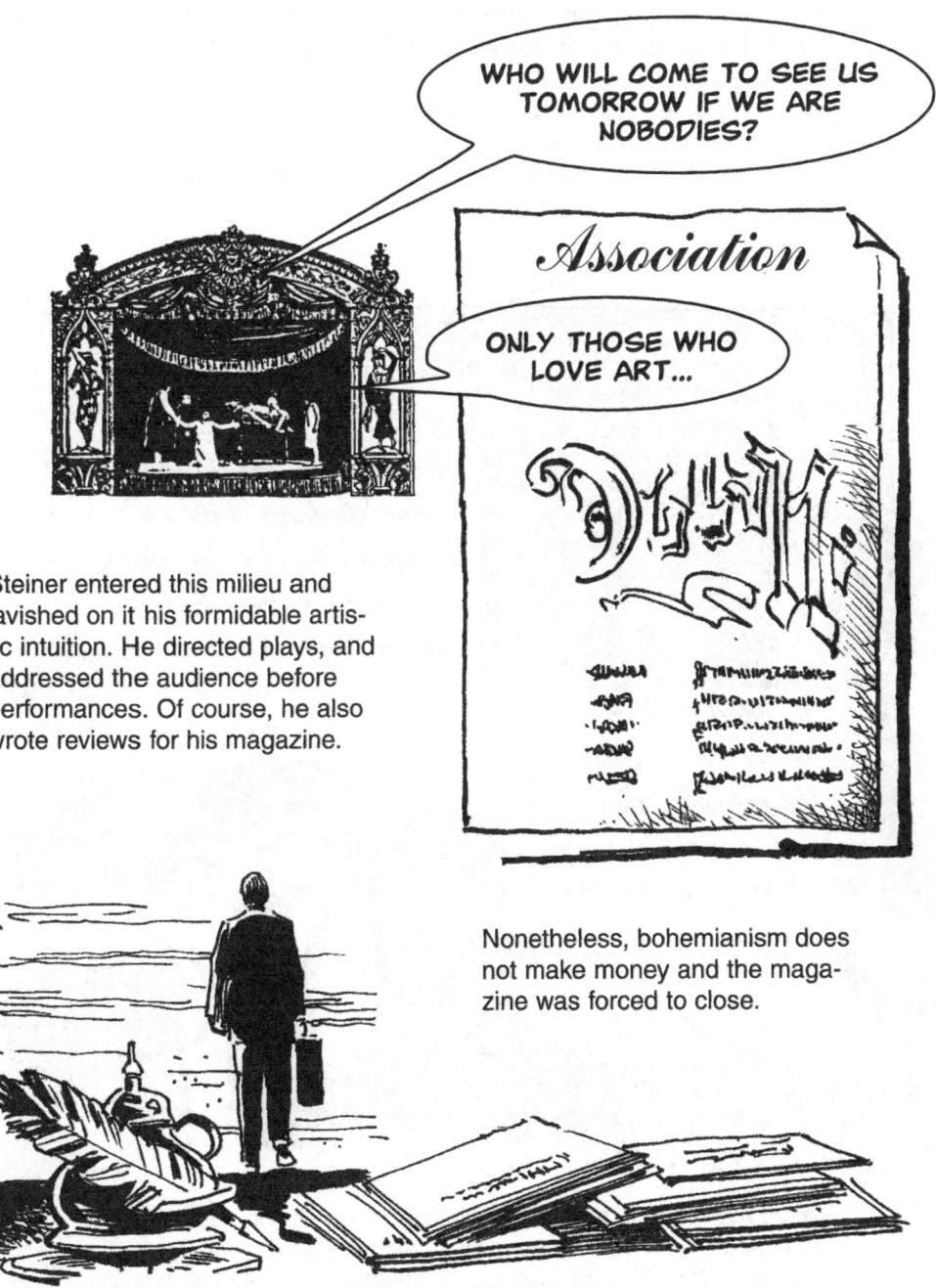

WHO WILL COME TO SEE US TOMORROW IF WE ARE NOBODIES?

ONLY THOSE WHO LOVE ART...

Steiner entered this milieu and lavished on it his formidable artistic intuition. He directed plays, and addressed the audience before performances. Of course, he also wrote reviews for his magazine.

Nonetheless, bohemianism does not make money and the magazine was forced to close.

This contact with the theatre had, however, planted its seeds.

When one field of activity seemed to close, another would open: Berlin's labour movement invited Steiner to teach in its **School for the Education of Workers**. He had one condition: that no political affiliation should be required of him and he should be allowed absolute ideological freedom. He taught history, cosmology, human anatomy, the social life of animals and oratory.

The political affiliation of the 'students' had no meaning for me, but their spiritual make-up did.

I needed to discern the ideas and values of these people and express myself in ways that were entirely foreign to me until then.

Steiner managed to enthuse his listeners; increasing numbers of students attended his classes, which were held five evenings a week, from 9 to 11, and even past midnight, after they had worked ten- or twelve-hour shifts.

His ascendancy over the workers reached a high point in a speech he was asked to deliver on Gutenberg's 500th anniversary: on 17 June 1900, Steiner spoke (without a microphone) in a Berlin auditorium, to 7,000 typographers. His words were met with lively enthusiasm.

However, the Party authorities felt threatened by the impulse toward freedom that Steiner encouraged in this generation of socialists in order to shake them out of their Marxist, materialist, cubby-holes. After five years of fruitful labour, they decided to dismiss him.

The Magazin fur Literature, forced me to become immersed in the bourgeois world and my job with the workers, in the proletarian world; fertile areas where one could acquire personal experience of the forces driving the times.

I have the impression that if at that time a greater number of unprejudiced persons had observed with interest the workers' movement, and if the proletariat had been treated with understanding, that movement would have developed in a very different way. But each one lived inside his own class, abandoning the other to live inside his. The concepts one class had about another were purely theoretical.

At that same time, the 'superior classes' lost touch with the feelings of the community, and along with savage competition, selfishness spread. Progressively, all links between the classes were broken.

At the same time, Steiner was invited on a regular basis to speak to groups of the most diverse intellectuals.

'The process is always the same: Steiner becomes part of the group in a human and spiritual sense, works actively, meets with approval and opposition, becomes one of them, yet continues to be a visitor among them, well-liked though a stranger. Nobody catches the more intimate connotations of his message...'

Only when he was invited to explain his ideas to 'theosophical circles' did Rudolf Steiner find an audience that was receptive to his way of thinking.

49

Theosophy

Founded in New York in 1875 by the Russian **Helena Petrovna Blavatsky** and the Englishman **Henry Steel Olcott**, the **Theosophical Society** eventually established its headquarters in Adyar, near Madras, in India, a testimony to its veneration for the ancient wisdom of that country.

The aims of the Theosophical Society were:

- the brotherhood of all men;
- the comparative study of religions;
- research into inexplicable natural phenomena, also through the use of extrasensory faculties.

According to theosophy, the development of mankind takes place in the framework of a divine evolutionary plan which offers—through the chain of the individual's reincarnations—a growing possibility of unlocking the divine life inhabiting the human 'form'.

The 'elder brothers' would already have reached the goal of human development and could help mankind through their occult knowledge, inspiring human progress and forming, with their teaching, the esoteric nucleus of the great religions.

Theosophy does not aspire to be a new religion, but to transmit ancestral spiritual ideas.

As a student in Vienna, Steiner had read **A.P. Sinett**'s *Esoteric Buddhism*, and **Mabel Collins**' *Light for the Way*, fundamental books on theosophy.

Just before leaving Vienna, he had attended a meeting of the recently-formed Theosophical Group.

In Berlin too a theosophical circle began to coalesce around **Count** and **Countess Brockdorff**. It was they who—after reading Steiner's book on Nietzsche—asked him to speak at their 'Theosophical Library'.

Although this was, at that time, the only group of people whose interest in worlds that the senses cannot perceive coincided with that of Steiner, the differences in their respective searches regarding form and content were deep and fundamental.

There were fundamental differences between theosophy and Steiner's thinking:

Theosophy	*Rudolf Steiner*
Seeks to approach the spiritual through spiritual and mediumistic practices.	Seeks to approach the spiritual through a rigorous and methodical investigation.
Reduced clarity of consciousness, similar to a trance state.	Increased clarity of consciousness.
Transmits ancient initiatory knowledge.	Admits only knowledge proven through his own rigorous and methodical investigation.
Keeps spiritual knowledge secret: 'esoteric'.	Seeks to communicate spiritual knowledge: 'exoteric'.
Favours the wisdom of the East.	Admires Eastern wisdom but does not believe it capable of solving the problems of the West. Definitely subscribes to western thought.
Seeks the integration of all religions.	Grants special meaning to the figure of Christ.
Establishes no relationship whatever with art.	Assigns fundamental importance to art.
Grants no importance to the historical vision.	Always offers the historical context.

Despite the differences, theosophical circles turned out to offer Steiner the most receptive environment for his thought and allowed him to establish the basis for his future action.

At first, Steiner used Hindu theosophical terminology to make himself understood. Later he looked for words more in tune with the modern western consciousness. In his first lecture at the Theosophical Library in September, 1900, he spoke about Nietzsche, whose tortured existence had reached an end a month before.

Later he spoke about 'Goethe's Occult Revelation'.

From that time onward, he spoke on a regular basis to this audience: in 1901 he gave a course spanning 27 evenings, later published as **Mysticism at the Dawn of the Modern Age**. The following year he gave 25 lectures that were also subsequently published as a book, **Christianity as Mystical Fact** (1902). Both works constitute the 'preamble' to anthroposophy.

In the second book, Steiner described how the great mystics of antiquity—and not only the Jewish prophets—were, basically, all preparing for the coming of Christ. That is: of a cosmic and divine being over the earth.

With this, Steiner placed himself in total opposition to the teachings of the Theosophical Society, according to which, Christ was considered one of the 'masters of wisdom' and not even the most significant among them.

Marie Von Sivers

Marie von Sivers just 'appeared one day' at one of Steiner's lectures. She later became his second wife, his most devoted student, his closest associate for the rest of his life and the worthy and active heiress to his work.

> WHO WILL PROVIDE AN ANSWER TO MY MOST INTIMATE SEARCH FOR THE TRUTH?

Marie von Sivers (1867-1948)

Born in Russia of an aristocratic family, Marie von Sivers was well-educated. She read and wrote Russian, German, English, French and Italian with equal ease. To enhance her remarkable innate talent, she studied theatre and recitation with several teachers in Europe.

> THEOSOPHY DOES NOT FULLY SATISFY ME, BUT WHAT STEINER SAYS IS MAGNETIC.

After the two series of lectures at the Brockdorffs' Library, in 1902 the Theosophical Society decided to establish a German branch and asked Steiner to become General Secretary. He accepted, subject to having the help of Marie von Sivers and also to being quite free to act according to his principles in his branch.

No-one was in any doubt that at the Theosophical Society I would reveal only the results of my own observation and research, for I emphasised this every time I had the opportunity.

I was not devoted to any sectarian dogma. I was only expressing what I myself experienced as a spiritual world.

At this branch, I was then able to develop my anthroposophical activity before an audience which constantly grew.

Despite Steiner's determination to make public spiritual knowledge that had previously been kept hidden, everything he presented, all his suggestions, the institutions he created, were all responses to some other person's concrete concern. He never offered information unless someone asked the relevant question.

In the autumn of 1901, on an anniversary of the international foundation of the Theosophical Society, an acquaintance of Countess Brockdorff invited the members of the Berlin branch to a commemorative tea known as the Chrysanthemum tea because there were so many of those flowers...

IT WAS AN UNEVENTFUL AFFAIR, EXCEPT FOR A CONVERSATION BETWEEN RUDOLF STEINER AND MARIE VON SIVERS.

WOULD IT BE POSSIBLE TO CREATE A SPIRITUAL MOVEMENT BASED ON THE EUROPEAN TRADITION AND THE IMPETUS OF CHRIST?

With this, I was given the opportunity to act in a way that I had only previously imagined. The question had been put to me, and now, according to spiritual laws, I could begin to answer it.

The birth of anthroposophy

As of that moment, Rudolf Steiner's biography was indissolubly linked—internally and externally—to the spiritual impulse which at that time was still generally known as 'theosophical', though often he already called it 'anthroposophical'.

'Anthroposophy is the consciousness of my humanity.'

IN GREEK:

SOFIA = WISDOM
THEOS = GOD
ANTHROPOS = MAN

The term '**anthroposophy**' was not new. It had previously been used by other philosophers. Yet it acquired its particular significance in relation to Rudolf Steiner's life and work.

During the first quarter of the twentieth century—the years remaining to him—Steiner worked tirelessly to consolidate anthroposophy as a spiritual science, as an art form and as a social stimulus.

AND WHAT WAS MARIE VON SIVERS' GREATEST ACCOMPLISHMENT?

TO ENDURE FOR 23 YEARS THE PACE DR STEINER SET AT WORK, WHICH WOULD HAVE EXHAUSTED THE REST OF US AFTER ONLY TWO WEEKS!

During all those years, Marie accompanied him and helped him as secretary, translator, editor and organiser of lectures, tours, interviews and artistic activities. Unconditionally devoted to Steiner's work, she also gave her life to anthroposophy, until her death in 1948.

Distinct phases can be seen in Steiner;s work:

1902–1909: Consolidation of anthroposophy as a spiritual science.

1910–1916: Consolidation of the artistic dimension.

1919–1923: Establishment of specific movements and institutions.

1924–1925: Consolidation of the Anthroposophical Society as a world-wide movement.

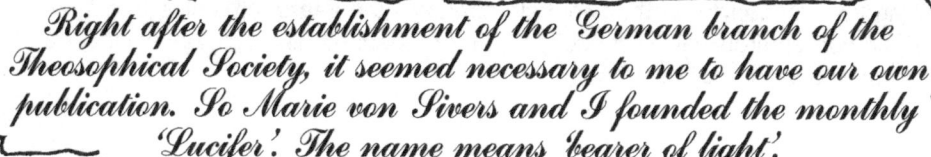

Right after the establishment of the German branch of the Theosophical Society, it seemed necessary to me to have our own publication. So Marie von Sivers and I founded the monthly 'Lucifer'. The name means 'bearer of light'.

Marie von Sivers made all this possible thanks to material sacrifice, insofar as possible, and by placing all her capacity for work in the service of anthroposophy.

At first, we really had to work in more than primitive conditions. I wrote most of 'Lucifer'. Marie von Sivers took charge of the letters. When each edition was finished, we wrapped it ourselves, wrote out the addresses, stuck the stamps on and personally delivered all the copies to the post office in a clothes basket.

Steiner's work in Berlin as a speaker to theosophical circles and to other audiences became more intensive.

Soon he was also in demand in other German cities, where affiliates of the Theosophical Society were being created.

Then London, Paris, Amsterdam, Rome, Budapest were added, and tours through Scandinavia.

The demands of tours and lectures grew so great, that it became impossible for him to continue the monthly publication of *Lucifer*, which had generated a great deal of interest.

And so a strange situation arose: a magazine whose subscribers grew minute by minute ceased publication, simply because its editor had too much work.

Marie von Sivers founded the **Philosophical-Theosophical Press** (later Philosophical-Anthroposophical) in Berlin to publish Rudolf Steiner's work, the task to which she would devote herself until the end of her life.

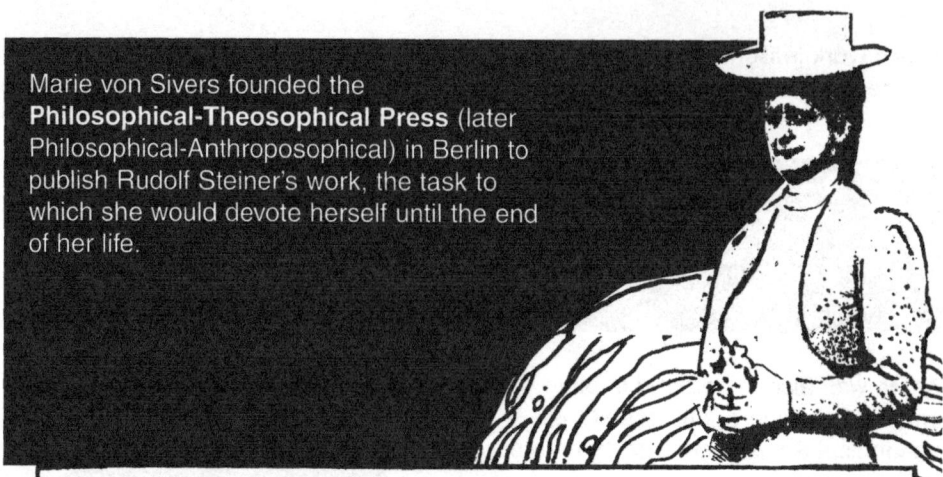

The bases for the anthroposophical ideas, set forth in many series of lectures during those early years and in the articles in the magazine *Lucifer*, are the contents of Steiner's classic books.

THEOSOPHY (1904)

HOW TO KNOW HIGHER WORLDS (1904)

AN OUTLINE OF OCCULT SCIENCE (1910)

The twentieth century dawned. Rudolf Steiner was forty years old.

He began to build, step by step, the ideological edifice of his **Spiritual Science**.

The book *Theosophy* (1904) established the basic pillars of this edifice:

• the image of man in his relation to nature;

• reincarnation and karma;

• 'the path of knowledge'.

The realms of nature

Steiner described living beings forming a pyramid, in which every realm of nature contributed a new element:

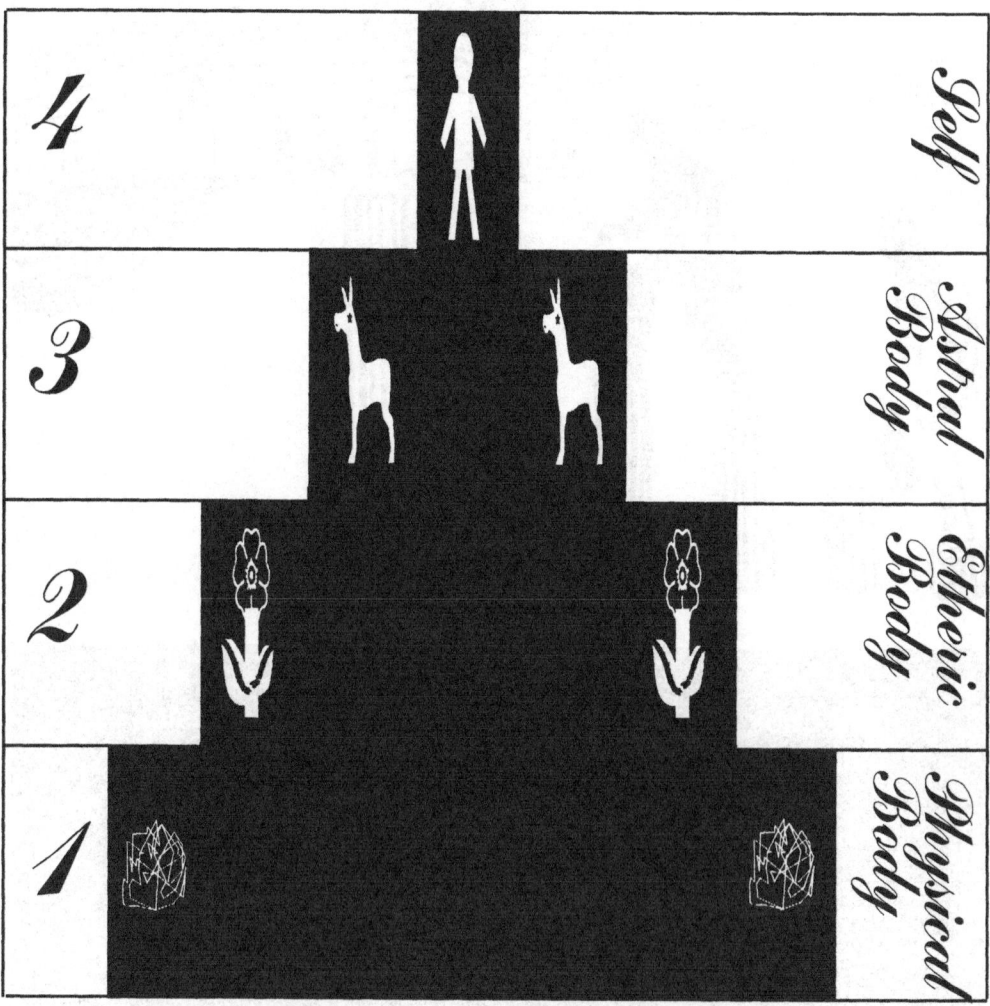

From the **mineral realm** comes the inert substance that makes up the **physical body** of all living beings: that part of them which, upon dying, returns to the mineral world, disintegrating.

 From the **vegetable realm** onwards, all beings possess what Steiner calls the **etheric body**, consisting of the vital or formative forces that ultimately shape the physical body and keep it alive.

 From the **animal realm** onwards, the animate element is added; animals not only live and reproduce, but they also have sensations and instincts, sympathies and antipathies. Rudolf Steiner calls this 'animal soul' (Aristotle) the **astral body**.

 The **self** belongs exclusively to the human being. It is what enables us to constitute ourselves as individuals, know ourselves and know our surroundings, alter the world. It gives us our specifically human faculties: the ability to walk upright, to speak, and to have the kind of thought that goes beyond reactions to momentary stimuli. It is the spiritual nucleus of the human being.

The image of man

The Western Christian tradition reduces the vision of man to a dichotomy between body and soul, devaluing the 'earthly body' in favour of the 'celestial soul'.

Because it holds that any existence can be reduced to matter or to an attribute or effect of materiality, **materialism** sees the human being only as a body, and tries to explain all psychical processes through physical and chemical changes in the nervous organism.

Rudolf Steiner's spiritual science understood the human being to be a trichotomy of body, soul and spirit.

To our senses, only the physical bodies of the world are perceptible. The remaining three 'bodies' described in anthroposophy (etheric body, astral body and self) are the 'packaging' of the physical body. They are 'supra-sensory' (imperceptible to the senses).

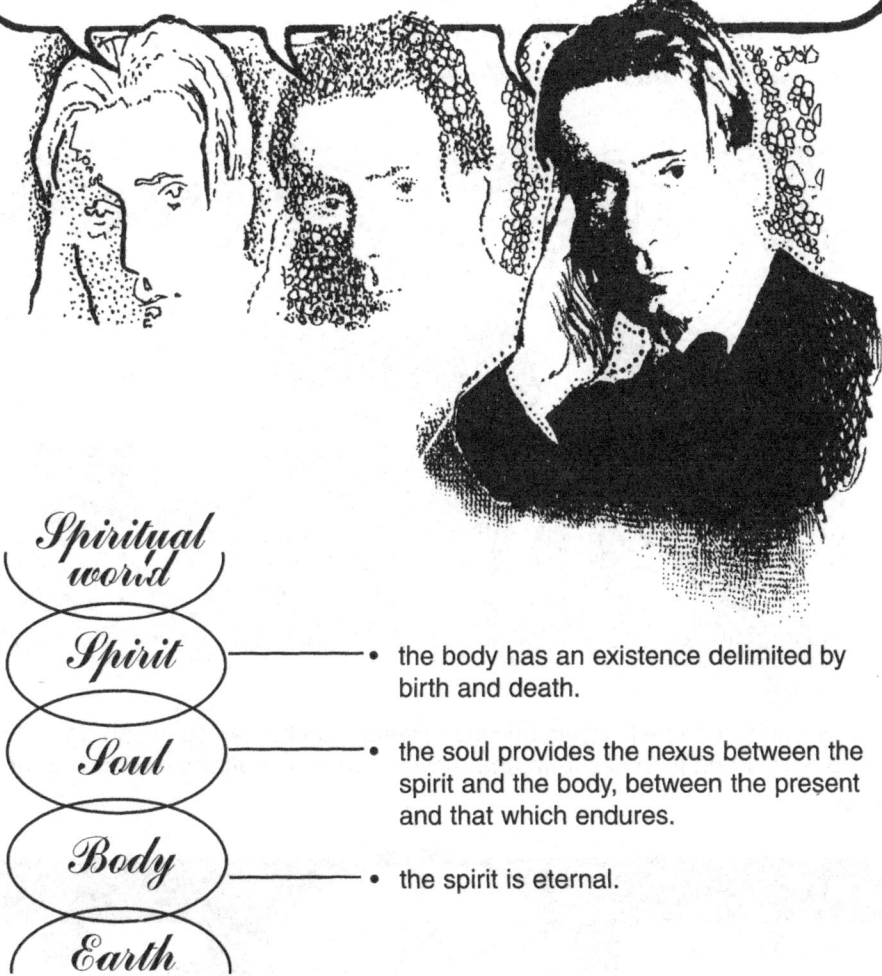

Man is a citizen of three worlds: through his body he belongs to the world he perceives through his physical senses; through his soul he builds his own world; through the spirit he accedes to a world which transcends the other two.

- the body has an existence delimited by birth and death.
- the soul provides the nexus between the spirit and the body, between the present and that which endures.
- the spirit is eternal.

Through the body's organs, the soul receives impressions of the world. These vanish when sensory perception ceases; however, they acquire an enduring effect through memory. Thus, animate life transforms the external world into an internal world, the instant into an enduring effect. And from that animate life, from the experiences that are undergone, the spirit in turn draws sustenance.

Rudolf Steiner used the image of water to describe the relationship between matter and spirit:

> *Just as an ice floe in the ocean is of the substance of the surrounding water, differentiated from the immediate environment through particular properties, objects perceived by the senses are of the substance of the surrounding animate-spiritual world and are differentiated from it through particular properties which make them perceptible to the senses.*

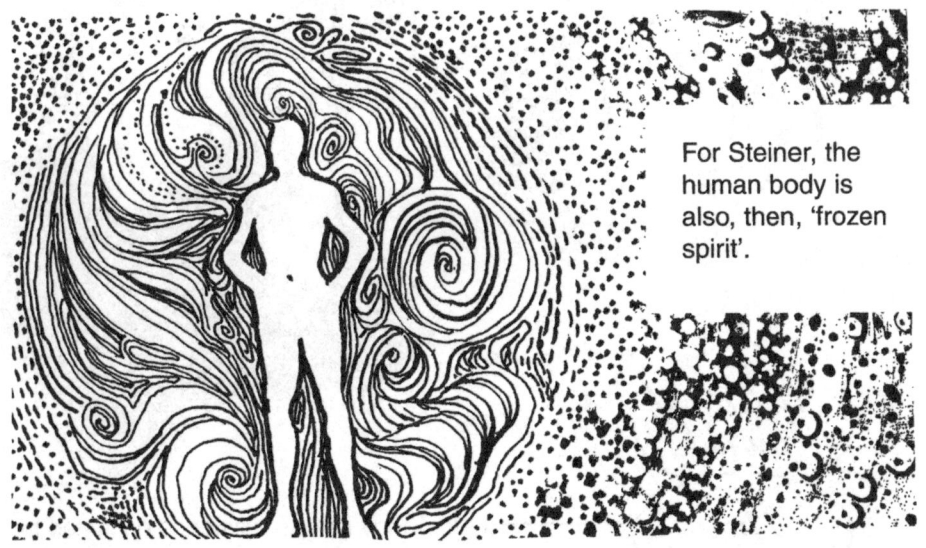

For Steiner, the human body is also, then, 'frozen spirit'.

Just as the ice can melt, again becoming water, the human spirit can again fuse into the spiritual world it comes from and—given certain conditions—condense again into bodily form.

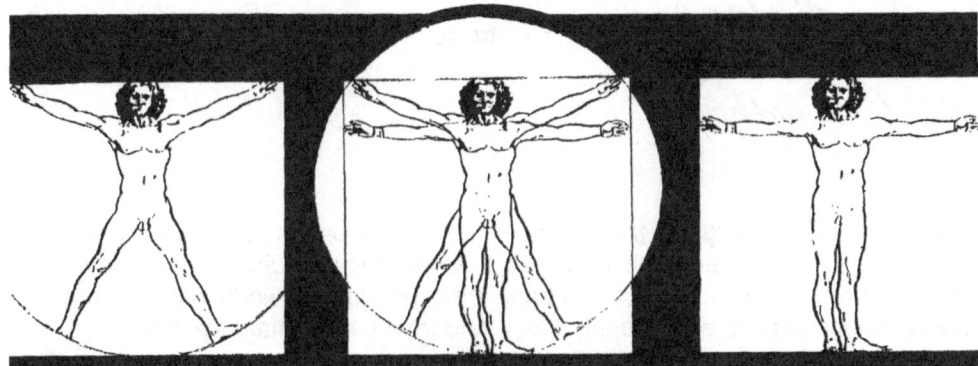

According to the anthroposophical concept, the human spirit is not a finished entity, but one in permanent evolution.

Man is not man, but he is becoming man.

The ideal of his development is full freedom. To achieve this goal, the human being must still undergo a long evolution.

Man is not free; he is on the way to freedom.

He conquers his freedom inasmuch as he becomes aware of the interrelations of the universe.

Every lesson learned is a freedom gained.

The evolution of the individual

Steiner applied the theory of the evolution of species, developed by Darwin in a materialistic sense, to man's spiritual entity.

IN TERMS OF THE PHYSICAL BEING THERE IS A SINGLE HUMAN SPECIES. IN A SPIRITUAL SENSE, EACH HUMAN BEING IS A COMPLETE SPECIES.

A BEING WHO CAN CALL HIM- SELF 'I' IS A COMPLETE WORLD...

THE HUMAN BEING IS MORE THAN AN EXEMPLAR OF THE HUMAN GENUS. HE SHARES HIS GENERIC CHARACTERIS- TICS WITH HIS PHYSICAL ANCESTORS, JUST LIKE ANI- MALS DO. BUT WHERE THE GENERIC ENDS, THERE BEGINS FOR MAN THAT WHICH DETERMINES HIS SPECIAL POSITION, HIS MISSION IN THE WORLD. THERE, ANY POS- SIBILITY OF AN EXPLANATION ACCORDING TO THE SCHEME OF PHYSICAL-ANIMAL INHERITANCE ENDS: I CAN RELATE SCHILLER'S NOSE OR A HAIR, PERHAPS EVEN CERTAIN TEMPERAMENTAL TRAITS, TO EQUIVALENTS AMONG HIS ANCESTORS, BUT NOT HIS GENIUS.

Each individual—and not only mankind as a whole—must have the possibility of working his way toward full consciousness, full freedom, full humanity.

> For this, he requires possibilities of evolution which are infinitely greater than those that fit into a single human life. The spirit must reincarnate in a succession of existences on earth: only here, through the physical organs, can he draw sustenance from experiences which permit him to advance, taking the fruits of one life to the next. That is how the individual destiny is constituted.

Thus, Rudolf Steiner concluded:

The body responds to the law of inheritance. The soul responds to the self-imposed destiny, karma. And the spirit responds to the law of reincarnation.

Reincarnation and karma

Karma (Sanskrit): to do, to act, to create.

An analogy can be made between the concept of reincarnation and sleep:

IN ANTHROPOSOPHICAL TERMS, WHEN A PERSON SLEEPS, HIS SELF AND HIS ASTRAL BODY DETACH THEMSELVES: WHAT LIES SLEEPING IS THE PHYSICAL BODY, WITH ITS VITAL FUNCTIONS (ETHERIC BODY).

AWAKENING IMPLIES THE RETURN OF CONSCIOUSNESS. WITH IT, THE THREAD OF EXPERIENCES AND THE CONSEQUENCES OF THE PREVIOUS DAY'S ACTS ARE AGAIN TAKEN UP.

When a person dies, the three higher 'bodies' detach themselves: the self, the astral body and the etheric or vital body. Only the corpse remains, now subject to the laws of the purely physical world.

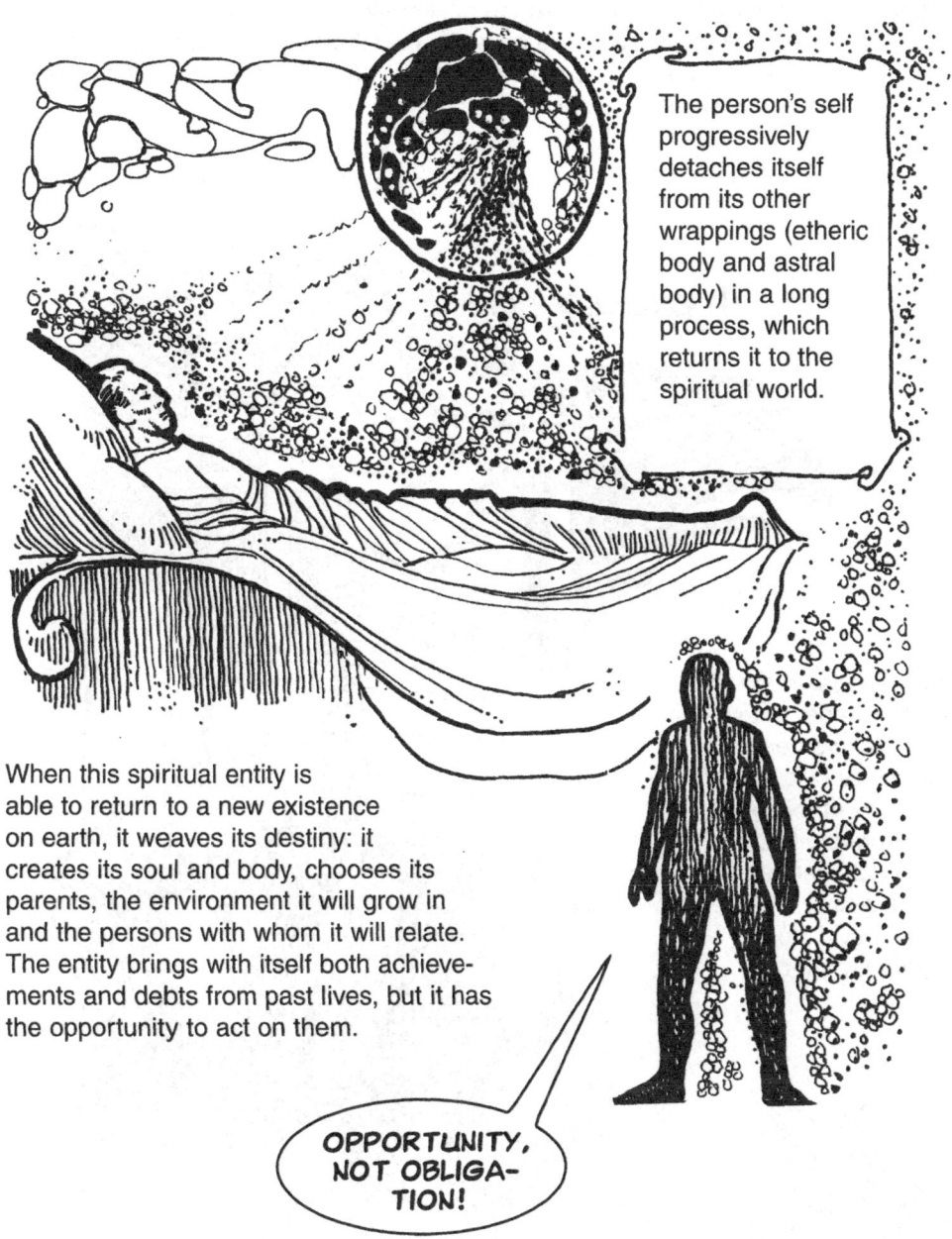

The person's self progressively detaches itself from its other wrappings (etheric body and astral body) in a long process, which returns it to the spiritual world.

When this spiritual entity is able to return to a new existence on earth, it weaves its destiny: it creates its soul and body, chooses its parents, the environment it will grow in and the persons with whom it will relate. The entity brings with itself both achievements and debts from past lives, but it has the opportunity to act on them.

OPPORTUNITY, NOT OBLIGATION!

In opposition to the fatalistic eastern vision, Steiner's vision of karma was based on the idea of the freedom of the human being.

The idea of reincarnation has quite often appeared in history: in the East it was always part of the great religions. Later, the theosophy of the nineteenth century brought it to the West.

Originally, Christianity also considered the possibility of the migration of souls through successive reincarnations. Afterwards, the Church waged a harsh war against this belief—held dear by so many heretics!—and eradicated it definitively from its doctrine at a Council in 529.

Nevertheless, in the history of Europe, many great thinkers declared themselves in favour of the theory of reincarnation: Giordano Bruno, Arthur Schopenhauer, Doris Lessing, Goethe, Fichte, David Hume, Richard Wagner...

With reference to reincarnation, Rudolf Steiner emphasised—and did so insistently throughout his entire body of work—that everything he expressed was derived directly from his own immediate spiritual experience. When he spoke of the different 'bodies' of the human being and in concrete terms of what happened to them after death, it was because he had observed and studied these realities with as much exactitude as a scientist in his laboratory.

In Steiner's fundamental books we find no reference to the reincarnations of any one particular individual. He was always vehemently opposed to the slightest hint of sensationalism in any topic he examined. Only at the end of his life, when his audience had already taken in the concepts themselves, did he decide to speak out about individual examples.

With grave warnings but with humour too, he rejected people who nagged him to discover who they had been in previous lives.

THEY ALL BELIEVE THEMSELVES TO BE THE REINCARNATION OF SOME GREAT PERSONAGE. THE FAVOURITE ONE IS MARY MAGDALENE.

AND TO THINK THAT I WAS ALEXANDER THE GREAT!

I WAS THE HIGH PRIESTESS OF ISIS.

AND I... I DON'T REMEMBER WHO I WAS!

The human aura

In Theosophy, Rudolf Steiner also tried to describe what he 'saw' with his 'spiritual eye' as the human aura.

Certainly, he was careful to warn that 'these things are not only difficult to observe, but especially difficult to describe'.

With extreme caution, he sought to explain the extremely subtle colour-sensations he perceived around a person according to his or her temperament, degree of spiritual evolution, mood, thoughts; he even observed variations in the form of the aura depending on the precision of thoughts...

But at the same time, there was no intention of 'exhibiting' his 'power'.

I SEE FROM YOUR AURA THAT YOU HAVE COMMITTED A CRIME!

ALL THIS HAS NOTHING TO DO WITH THE DOUBTFUL ART OF INTERPRETING HUMAN SOULS FROM THEIR AURAS...

For the contemporary way of thinking, anthroposophical ideas may have seemed fantastic and even absurd.

Their creator did not aspire to being believed—on the contrary, he always energetically resisted any blind faith placed in his 'authority', any dogmatism or sectarianism.

He appealed to his reader's freedom and conscience; his aim was to provide the reader with proposals, the truth of which he could examine and evaluate himself.

• The results of the natural sciences are based on perception by the physical senses. These were given to us at birth.

• The results of the spiritual sciences are based on 'extra-sensory perception'. Very few individuals evince an innate capacity to 'see' beyond visible phenomena.

Rudolf Steiner believed, however, that all human beings possess 'supra-sensory organs'. In the present evolutionary stage of mankind, all individuals may not have these at their disposal; however, such 'organs' can be developed by anyone willing to do so.

The path of knowledge

The book ***Theosophy*** ends with an initial description of the conditions to 'open the spiritual eye of the human being'. Later Rudolf Steiner developed this theme in greater detail in ***How to Know Higher Worlds***.

Steiner proposed intensifying—through a long and intense process of exercise and meditation—the conscious management of the powers of thought: by freeing consciousness from its bondage to the physical-sensory world, it could be led to an 'empty' state, but equally an awakened one, receptive to a new clairvoyance...

With *How to Know Higher Worlds* (1904-1909), Rudolf Steiner took a fundamental step in carrying out his decision to explain publicly what had hitherto been the 'occult knowledge' of a few initiates.

Convinced that—after conquering the natural sciences—human beings would be compelled to explore the spiritual sciences, Steiner described the method through which he was able to gain the spiritual knowledge that was the basis of all his work.

The proposed path demands of the disciple enormous energy and perseverance, to gain mastery over thoughts, feelings and will. Despite this, according to Steiner there is not a single person who cannot tread this path, if he is really determined.

Conditions to acquire knowledge of the higher worlds:

In every human being capacities lie slumbering, through which he can gain access to higher worlds...

Only within his own soul can the human being find the means that will open the way to spiritual knowledge.

Each human being carries inside, along with his everyday being, a higher being. It remains hidden until awakened. And only the individual himself can have access to it.

The book describes in a concrete manner the steps leading to 'illumination' and 'initiation', to 'seeing' and 'listening' with the interior senses. Steiner indicated the exercises which—when performed on a regular basis and with patience—lead to the opening and maturation of the corresponding 'organs'.

During the entire process a **golden rule** must be observed: for every step you endeavour to take to acquire occult truths, you must also take three steps in perfecting your character toward what is good.

In this sense, *How to Know Higher Worlds*, as much as a book on spiritual initiation, is a guide to consolidating one's own mental health. Steiner's principal tasks are given as follows:

- cultivate a devotion for **truth** and **knowledge**;

- learn to differentiate between what is **essential** and what is not;

- struggle against your own prejudices;

- learn to stand firmly and with unconditional **honesty** before yourself, and also before a perfect stranger;

- cultivate **inner peace**;

- exercise **patience** before expecting results;

- practice **respect** for others: do not criticise their defects but, with love, value their virtues. Your own acts and words must always take into account the **freedom** of the other;

- be reserved: do not boast of your achievements nor impose your own 'wisdom' on whoever has not shown himself willing to hear it;

- practice **humility**, knowing that one can always learn, even from the 'littlest' one (for example, and especially, from children);

- seek knowledge not to enrich yourself egoistically nor to obtain personal power, but in the awareness of participating in the evolutionary path of **mankind**.

After long and persistent training, an inner space opens to the 'spiritual student', a space where he can hold in suspension the existential questions, in patient expectation of an answer...

The Akashic Record

Steiner always sought to place the topics he discussed in a historical context. But his vision of the past also went beyond what was 'apparent':

Whoever has earned the capacity to perceive the spiritual world, will find in it the eternal character of what happened in the past. Everything will appear before him, not like the dead testimonies of history, but fully alive. He will be able to direct his retrospective view toward a past far more remote than the periods of external history.

In ancient India, this etheric-astral register of the Earth was called the '**Akashic Record**'.

Steiner adopted this name and gave innumerable proofs of how complete and concrete were his visions of the past, the present and even the future of mankind.

WHAT WAS HUMANITY LIKE WHEN THERE STILL EXISTED BETWEEN AMERICA AND EUROPE THE CONTINENT OF ATLANTIS, WHOSE LAST REMAINS SANK INTO THE OCEAN IN ABOUT 10,000 BC?

...The Atlanteans mastered the 'vital force'. Just as in the present we extract from coal heat that is transformed into locomotive force in our means of transportation, the Atlanteans were capable of putting to work the germinative force of living beings. In the time of Atlantis, plants were grown not only for food but also to place their latent force in the service of transportation and industry. That is how they managed to power vehicles that flew just a few feet over the surface of the earth. We must remember that in those days the atmosphere was much less dense: today these vehicles would be quite useless...

An Outline of Occult Science

In this third 'pillar' of anthroposophical thought, **An Outline of Occult Science** (1910), Steiner discussed mainly the unfolding of the universe, the earth and man, just as it had been manifested to his 'supra-sensory' consciousness.

Steiner's cosmology

In *On the Origin of Species by means of Natural Selection* Darwin attempted a timid and 'not very scientific' answer to the question of the origin of life:

I HOLD THAT ALL ORGANIC BEINGS WHICH HAVE EVER EXISTED ON THIS EARTH DESCEND FROM A PRIMORDIAL FORM, IN WHICH LIFE WAS INSTILLED BY THE CREATOR.

Life can only come from life.

Later, materialistic science preferred to avoid this 'uncomfortable' sentence, and concentrated on laying the basis, step by step, of the physical evolution of nature and man, whose animate life would have developed only on the basis of his corporeality.

And the spirit can come only from a spiritual world.

According to Steiner, the human being's animate-spiritual existence can be traced right back to the origin of the cosmos, and is thus prior to the human's physical presence on earth.

Not only man, but also the earth and the entire cosmos have gradually undergone stages of progressive materialisation starting from their primordial spiritual state.

		Pure spirituality.	Time does not exist, only 'duration'.
Fire	1.	The existential seeds emerging from the spiritual world reach a state of heat, the first and very subtle manifestation of life.	TIME begins.
Air	2.	Gaseous forms arise, from which light emanates.	
Water	3.	The process of materialisation reaches the liquid state.	
Earth	4.	The solid state is reached. The earthly element proper arises. Sexual differentiation appears and—as the culmination of solidification—the possibility of death.	WE ARE NOW IN THIS FOURTH COSMIC STAGE.
	5. 6. 7.	Future stages of progressive spiritualisation.	

The birth of human individuality

Throughout the four evolutionary stages of human organisation, its consciousness has grown gradually as, one by one, the 'bodies' which make it up are integrated into it:

evolutionary stage	birth of	consciousness
1	physical body	merely nebulous
2	etheric body	**vegetative**, a state of dreamy innocence
3	astral body	**dream-like**, reflecting reality (the instincts appear)
4	self	**rational.** Birth of the independence of the human individuality

In the three stages which still remain to be experienced, the human self, through conscious work, must sublimate, one by one, its three inferior 'bodies', to once again reach—far into the future—the maximum degree of spirituality.

The 'natural sciences' recognise two determining factors of human individuality: the genetic factor (inheritance) and the cultural factor (environmental influences).

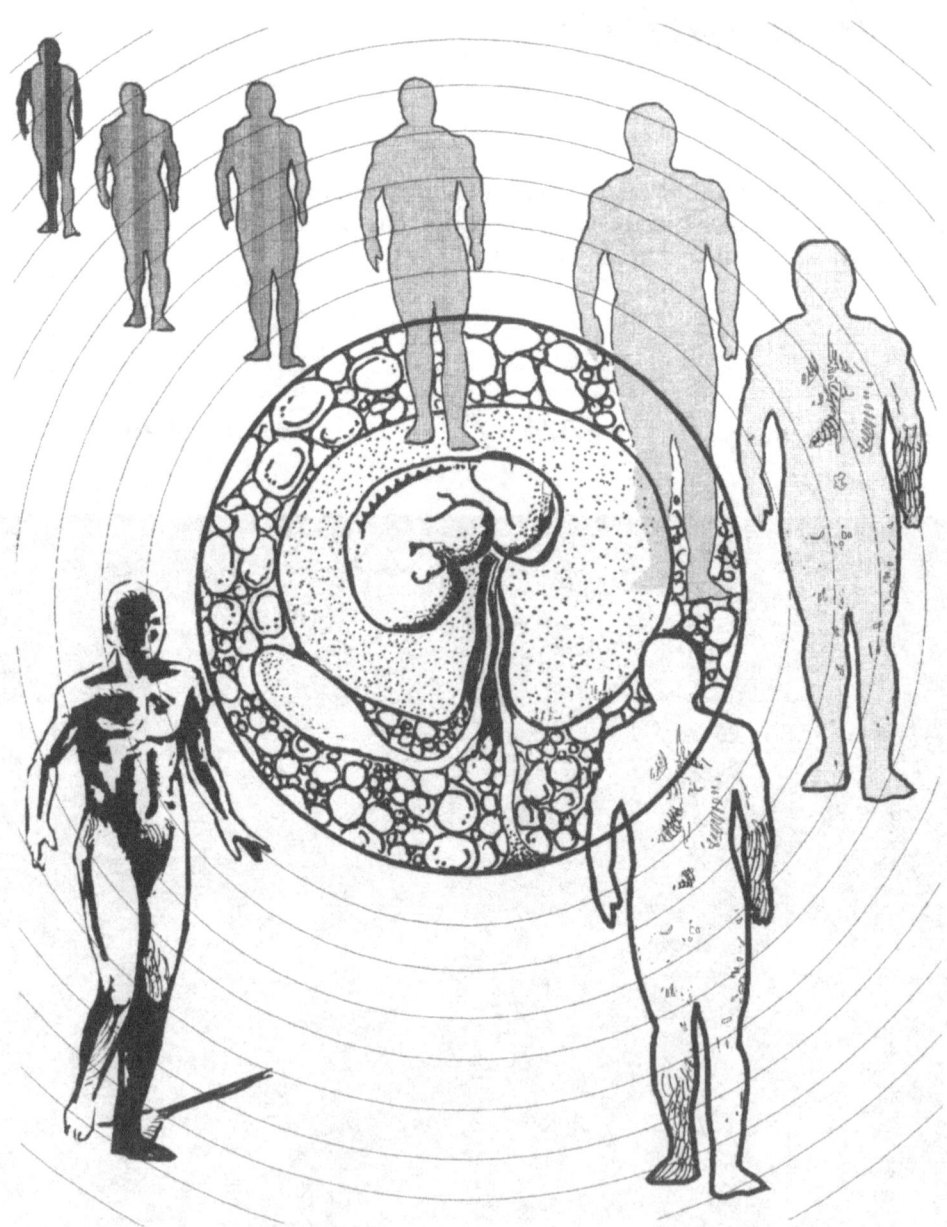

'Spiritual science', on the basis of the idea of reincarnation and karma, adds a third factor: the human self, which carries over from its pre-natal existence and from previous lives, conditioning that determines the absolutely unique qualities and circumstances of its life on earth.

With this view of human individuality, the endless argument about what influences the person most—nature (heredity) or nurture (culture)—becomes unimportant, and many other aspects of human existence begin to make more sense.

The '**moral sentiment**' is therefore inherent in the human being, (that is, the responsibility he assumes toward his fellow beings, toward nature, the future of the earth, etc.), because for the individual who is convinced that he did not ask to come into this hazardous world, and that he will leave it forever and with no consequences for himself, the logical consequence would be pure egoism.

- The search for the 'meaning of life': the individual who returns to the earth at different moments of history with a varied set of possibilities, is the maker of his own evolution and a participant in the evolution of mankind. He might feel much more on the way to a goal than one who seeks to close the circle of his destiny within the narrow confines of a single life.

- The 'injustices of life': physical or mental differences, premature death, the horrors and suffering which 'punish' particular persons, acquire new meaning with the opportunity to correct errors or omissions from past lives.

- 'Human relations': family, couples, friends—when relationships are no longer conceived as the results of chance, but as 'choices' of the self to continue work on tasks pending with other individuals, these are all ordered in a context of greater perspectives and responsibilities.

- The 'desire of man to perpetuate himself': compared to the attempt to freeze human bodies (an arguably laughable way of prolonging life), the idea of a succession of natural returns of the individual to earth until he 'does all his homework' opens up immeasurable possibilities.

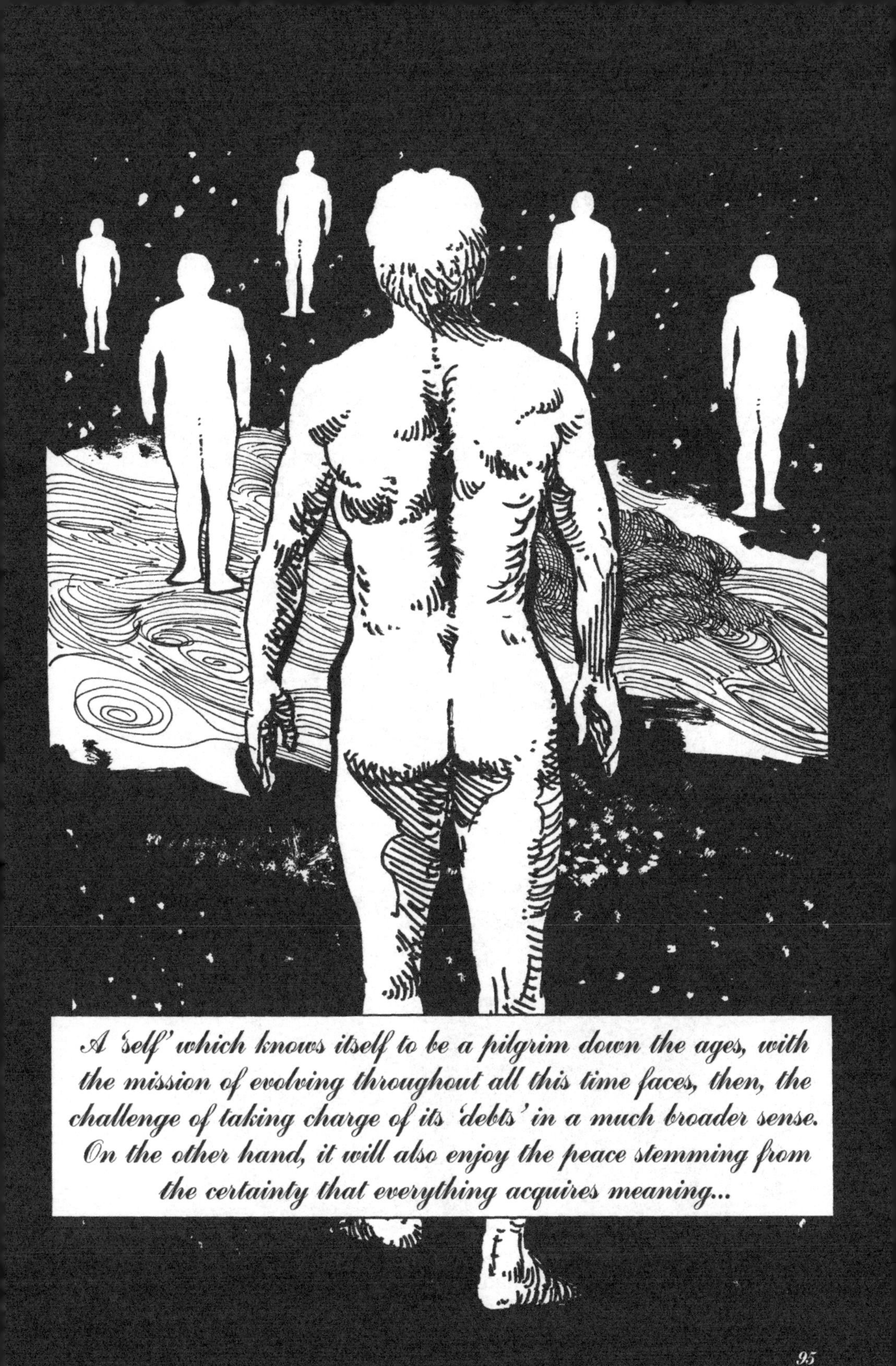

A 'self' which knows itself to be a pilgrim down the ages, with the mission of evolving throughout all this time faces, then, the challenge of taking charge of its 'debts' in a much broader sense. On the other hand, it will also enjoy the peace stemming from the certainty that everything acquires meaning...

Anthroposophy and Christianity

Rudolf Steiner described the time of his life when he struggled to clarify his attitude to Christ as a period when his soul faced difficult tests.

Once again he sought access, through his spiritual investigation, to an absolutely coherent inner vision. When he had achieved it, he began to discuss in lectures and books his thoughts on the life of Christ, the Gospels, the Apocalypse, etc.

Steiner described the 'Mystery of Golgotha' as a cosmic event which is the axis of all earthly evolution.

At the darkest moment of the history of the earth, Christ, a spiritual and divine being—the 'Word' or 'Logos'—was incarnated in the man Jesus of Nazareth, during the last three years of his life. As of this time, the strength of the 'Word', which until then had acted on the terrestrial sphere from without, began to be united with it, altering the aura of the earth.

CHRISTIANITY BEGAN AS A RELIGION, YET IT IS VASTER THAN ALL RELIGIONS.

Leaving aside all religious dogmas, this has meaning, according to Steiner, for all mankind and will be perceived by men when they are spiritually prepared.

Within the International Theosophical Society Rudolf Steiner found little understanding for his vision of the phenomenon of Christ as an absolutely unique event for humanity. In 1913, the insistence with which **Annie Besant**, the president and dominating personality of the Society, presented the child **Krishnamurti** as the new Messiah, made their differences all the more acute.

2nd phase of anthroposophy: the artistic impulse (1910-1916)

Another aspect distinguished anthroposophy from theosophy: the importance accorded to art. After the break, artistic expression came to life. Especially in colourful and romantic Munich, kaleidoscope of the artistic vanguard, those who attended Rudolf Steiner's courses were eager to see a closer relationship between art and anthroposophy.

Marie von Sivers drew on her artistic background and gave introductory poetry recitals at Steiner's lectures. Together, they developed a declamatory art which became quite important in the decades to follow.

The 'drama mysteries'

Between 1910 and 1913 Rudolf Steiner wrote and produced a 'drama mystery' for each season. These were not plays in a classical sense—they were the artistic representation of the central themes of anthroposophy: with thematic continuity throughout the four plays, the characters experienced the spiritual search through a succession of incarnations.

THESE THEATRICAL SEASONS IN MUNICH WERE THE LOVELIEST TIME OF EACH YEAR. THEN WE COULD CONCENTRATE FOR NEARLY TWO MONTHS ON A SINGLE TASK.

DURING THE DAY WE REHEARSED. AT NIGHT RUDOLF WROTE THE DRAMAS HE HAD ALREADY CONCEIVED IN HIS MIND. THEN HE VISITED THE WORKSHOPS WHERE, FOLLOWING HIS INSTRUCTIONS, PEOPLE WOULD BE SAWING, HAMMERING, PAINTING, MODELLING, SEWING AND EMBROIDERING.

With progress in theatrical work came his followers' wish to have their own theatre, with a large stage and space for other artistic and scientific activities.

In Munich, the authorities rejected the project which was presented to them, but Steiner received a donation: a plot of land on a hill in Dormach, close to Basel, Switzerland, where they managed to get their plans approved without difficulty. The centre of the anthroposophical movement was therefore built in the only country of Central Europe that did not participate in the two world wars...

The stormy night of 20 September fell as the cornerstone of the building was laid. Marie von Sivers recalled the scene:

THE WIND HOWLED, A TORRENT OF RAIN FELL, OUR FEET SANK IN THE MUD... LIGHT FROM THE GREAT TORCHES FLICKERED ON THE TRENCH WHERE THE STONE WAS TO BE SUNK...

THE LUGUBRIOUS SPELL CAST BY THE ELEMENTS SEEMED TO PRESAGE FUTURE STORMS... BUT STEINER'S WORD HELD SWAY WITH CLARITY AND GREATNESS...

The Goetheanum

The '**Goetheanum**' was the name given to the building, testimony once again to the close affinity between anthroposophy and Goethe's philosophy; especially Goethe's ideas about the metamorphosis of plants through a primordial formative principle inherent in the entire vegetable world, which was given form by Steiner in this work.

Because he was aware that the shape of the building needed to correspond in its minutest details to the work that was to be done in it, he created an entirely new language of forms, the result of the metamorphosis of the formative influences which act in nature.

That is why the architecture Steiner created—later applied to public and private buildings in the most diverse parts of the world—is called 'organic'.

Steiner modelled his projects in clay instead of drawing them on paper. He worked to solve both the technical problems the innovative design presented, and to conceive each detail in light of the building's concept as art.

Over a concrete base, two interlinked cupolas tiled in Norwegian slate were erected: the small one covered the stage, the large one a theatre for an audience of one thousand (in its day, Europe's largest theatre).

Held up by enormous columns of different kinds of wood, carved according to quite precise designs and instructions, the cupolas were painted with frescoes designed by Steiner; he also studied how to mix and apply special vegetable paints.

The great windows were made according to designs in bas relief filled in with thick coloured glass. Dentist's drills were brought from the United States for this job.

Architects and engineers of that time expressed their admiration for the solutions found to technical problems, especially the junction of the two cupolas. One renowned American architect said:

> WHOEVER WAS RESPONSIBLE FOR SOLVING THIS PROBLEM IS A MATHEMATICAL GENIUS OF THE HIGHEST ORDER... WE ARCHITECTS MUST LEARN FROM THIS. WHOEVER ERECTED IT CONQUERED THE HEIGHTS, BECAUSE HE HAS MASTERY OVER THE DEPTHS.

In the London *Times*, the English architect, Montague Wheeler, wrote:

'The man who built an edifice covered by two interlinked cupolas, the largest of which has a diameter greater than St. Peter's Basilica, deserves the most serious consideration from the practitioners of architecture... As an audacious step in the representation of a new architecture, this building will brook no rivals in the history of art.'

Construction proceeded at a dizzying speed...

The work was entirely financed by donations from friends of anthroposophy.

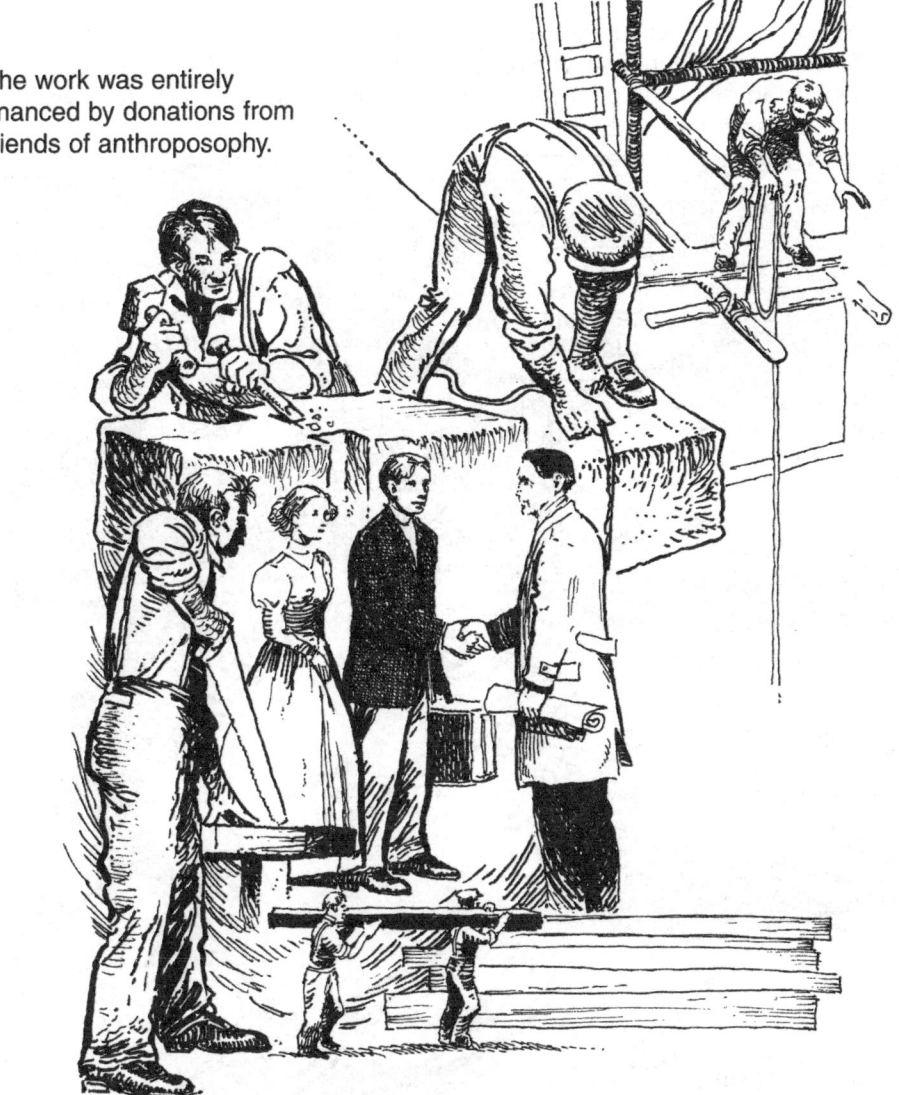

Besides many hired workmen, volunteers—people from many different professions and walks of life—came from all over the world, especially Germany. At great personal and economic sacrifice, they left their families and jobs to share workmen's barracks with other enthusiasts. Their hands became calloused from wielding hammer and chisel.

Steiner wanted the work finished by August of 1914, in order to stage the fifth drama mystery, already written in his mind. But external events intervened, inexorably...

In August 1914, World War I began

Rudolf Steiner and his entourage were at a performance of Wagner's *Parsifal* in Bayreuth, Germany, when the news reached them. They immediately left for Switzerland in an open car, protected from the ghostly night's cold by improvised coats. Apprehensively, they approached the border...

WHERE ARE YOU COMING FROM?

FROM BAYREUTH.

THESE ARE YOUR OPERA CLOTHES?

YES!

The barrier went up for them.

BEHIND US, A WORLD WAS SINKING INTO HARDSHIP AND DESOLATION, MARCHING TOWARDS ITS BLACKEST FATE. THIS WAS THE MOST PAINFUL DAY OF RUDOLF STEINER'S LIFE. I HAD NEVER SEEN HIM SO DOWNCAST.

The war created severe difficulties for the progress of the building, though it did not manage to dampen the enthusiasm of those who were participating.

While the world crumbled amid hatred and anguish, in Dormach volunteers from seventeen nations continued building their centre for anthroposophy.

From afar, behind the border, the rolling thunder of cannon could be heard... One by one, those men who were fit for service left to be drafted as soldiers in their own countries. Many never returned.

There are many stories told by the people who worked together building the Goetheanum. They agreed about the intensity of the experience they all shared. For his part, Rudolf Steiner was the 'content and container' of all that fervour.

WE HAD CONGREGATED IN A COMMUNITY THAT WAS TOTALLY NEW AND FREE. EACH WORKED IN HIS OWN WAY... ONLY THE AWARENESS OF PARTICIPATING IN A GREAT WORK FOR THE FUTURE, AND DR. STEINER'S HELP AND ORIENTATION, MADE ORDER OUT OF THIS CHAOS.

THE SPIRITUAL GREATNESS, HUMAN GOODNESS AND PRACTICAL SKILL OF RUDOLF STEINER ACHIEVED HARMONY AMONG ALL THOSE PEOPLE OF SUCH VARIED TALENTS AND INCLINATIONS.

FROM MORNING TO NIGHT I SAW HIM AT THE SITE, HIGH BOOTS AND OVERALLS COVERING HIS USUAL BLACK COAT.

...NOT ONLY DID HIS MASTERFUL SKILL AND PRECISION WHEN HANDLING TOOLS AND PAINTBRUSHES ASTOUND PEOPLE, BUT ALSO HIS AGILITY AND SUREFOOTEDNESS WHEN MOVING AROUND ON THE SCAFFOLDING AND AMONG PILES OF MATERIALS—AT 55 YEARS OF AGE...

For the back of the Goetheanum's stage, Steiner created a sculpture in wood, 9.5 metres high.

He named this great central figure the 'Representative of Humanity'. It was an image of Christ which was meant to express the personification of love with a gesture suggesting 'I judge not'.

One of the first buildings at Dornach was the so-called 'carpentry shop', a deposit for materials and at the same time the workshop where the large blocks of wood were assembled. Provisionally, the carpentry shop became the meeting place for all the participants. At the time, no-one suspected that it would continue to meet this need for many years to come.

Besides initiating his followers in the fundamentals of the new artistic impulses that were emerging in Dormach, Steiner continued to lecture systematically on the results of his spiritual search.

He also gave courses for the Goetheanum's workers, who attended them with increasing interest.

He made a special effort to mitigate the suffering caused by the war. He gave courses on first aid and also tried to comfort and give inner strength to those present, through meditations and a spiritual vision of events.

Eurythmy

At the behest of a young woman who wished to devote her life to an art of movement based on anthroposophical thought, Steiner created Eurythmy. Eurythmy—as with 'organic' architecture—aimed for an artistic expression of the plastic processes inherent in life. Eurythmy sought to make visible in human gestures and movements, the spiritual qualities of words and music: it was 'visible language' and 'visible music'.

As a way of externalising the 'laws' acting in nature, it also had its fixed rules, its obligatory gestures for each vowel, each consonant, each note, each interval...

ITS FORMS ARE NEITHER TRANSITORY NOR ARBITRARY, BUT COSMIC AND CHARGED WITH MEANING. THE HUMAN BEING IS A FINISHED FORM. BUT THAT FORM AROSE FROM MOVEMENT... EURYTHMY RECOVERS THE PRIMORDIAL MOVEMENTS WHICH CREATED MAN.

From its most elementary beginnings in 1912, eurythmy grew, with Steiner's continued creative contribution. During the war, two schools of eurythmy came into being, both under the tutelage of Marie von Sivers: one in Berlin and one in Dormach. At the latter, along with the work building the Goetheanum, a group of enthusiastic pioneers sought to perfect their practice of the new art. They even set up a stage in the carpentry shop for the first performances of eurythmy.

In time, eurythmy developed into three different branches:
- Artistic eurythmy;
- Educational eurythmy—applied in anthroposophical schools;
- Therapeutic eurythmy—intended to help anthroposophical medicine to establish balance where there were deviations in mind and body.

A new scenic art emerged when the experience of the 'drama mysteries' was brought together with eurythmy, the 'formation of speech' (meaning the artistic recitation developed by Steiner and Marie von Sivers, especially to accompany eurythmy), and the new movements in painting and sculpture and even music.

From 1915 onward, Steiner began to stage—in the precarious venue of the carpentry shop—parts of Goethe's *Faust*. This endeavour was crowned years after his death, when in 1938 the Goetheanum was the first stage in the world to present *Faust* in its complete form (because of its dramatic complexity, the play is generally abridged). From then on, this 'festival' was repeated year after year, with thousands of spectators attending from around the world.

From Dornach, where he established his (most) permanent residence, Steiner continued to travel through Europe (despite the difficulties created by the war), to speak to the growing number of people who awaited him eagerly or even followed him from town to town.

HE SPOKE FREELY WITH NO MANUSCRIPT OR NOTES. HIS LECTURES SEEMED TO SPRING FROM AN INNER DIALOGUE WITH THE AUDIENCE.

Steiner always spoke in German, with a translator present (one of the few deficiencies attributed to him was not speaking other languages). However, those who travelled with him from one country to another noted how the topics he chose and his way of speaking were adapted to the soul of each nation.

But the demands persisted. Unofficial copies did circulate, transcribed and translated, multiplying the inaccuracies. So Marie took charge and began to correct the shorthand versions and to print a number of series of lectures. Now the index of these publications alone fills a book.

1900

From Steiner's first lecture at the Brockdorffs' library in Berlin, considered the 'mother cell' of the anthroposophy, the movement, has grown vigorously.

Day by day, the number of people who found an answer to their deepest questions in Steiner's words grew, and they experienced their encounter with anthroposophy as a 'homecoming'.

They are those who are willing to 'start over', to get involved with making enormous efforts of all kinds as they walk on Steiner's 'path of knowledge', those who produce inward and outward growth in the 'edifice' of anthroposophy.

1920

By the time the first course was presented at the Goetheanum (the building was nearly finished), Steiner was able to address an audience that was quite advanced in the study of anthroposophy. The building then became, as well as a large-scale arts centre, 'The Higher Independent School of Spiritual Sciences'.

3rd Phase of Anthroposophy: practical applications (1917-1925)

The disciples also tried to make a reality of the master's constant invocation:

ANTHROPOSOPHY SHOULD NOT DISTANCE THE INDIVIDUAL FROM PRACTICAL LIFE; RATHER, IT SHOULD MAKE HIM MORE APT AND RESPONSIBLE FOR LIFE.

In this sense, each person tried to embody the new concept of the world in the everyday exercise of his or her profession, his or her social role.

NOW THAT RUDOLF STEINER RECEIVES REQUESTS FROM THE MOST VARIED FIELDS OF HUMAN ACTIVITY, HE CAN BEGIN TO ACT SPECIFICALLY IN EACH FIELD.

Thus began the third phase of anthroposophy: its practical uses and the derived movements.

The flags raised by World War I were those of democracy and nationalism, that of the right of peoples to self-determination. The struggle was a new wave in the great tide set in motion by the French Revolution.

At the end of the war in 1918, old Europe was devastated. Her long 'reign' over the rest of the world had ended. Many of her monarchies fell, giving way to democratic, parliamentary systems. New borders modified the political map of the entire continent.

The peace treaties pacified neither the victors nor the vanquished The new systems proved to be even more unstable; the new borders created nests of agitation and left millions of refugees to wander aimlessly. The social and economic order regressed deeply (most radically in Russia after the Bolshevik revolution of 1917). Deep pessimism became the predominant mood of people, a sense of the 'decadence of the West'.

The threefold structuring of the Social Organism

Right in the middle of the war, Steiner presented the concept of 'The threefold structuring of the Social Organism', affirming: 'Just as the human organism is organised in inter-dependent systems, the social organism too is made up of three systems. Each of them satisfies a type of need in the human being:

- physical needs are satisfied by the economy;
- psychological needs (the most basic of which is security), by the legal order (the state, politics);
- spiritual needs (education, science, art, religion), by cultural life.'

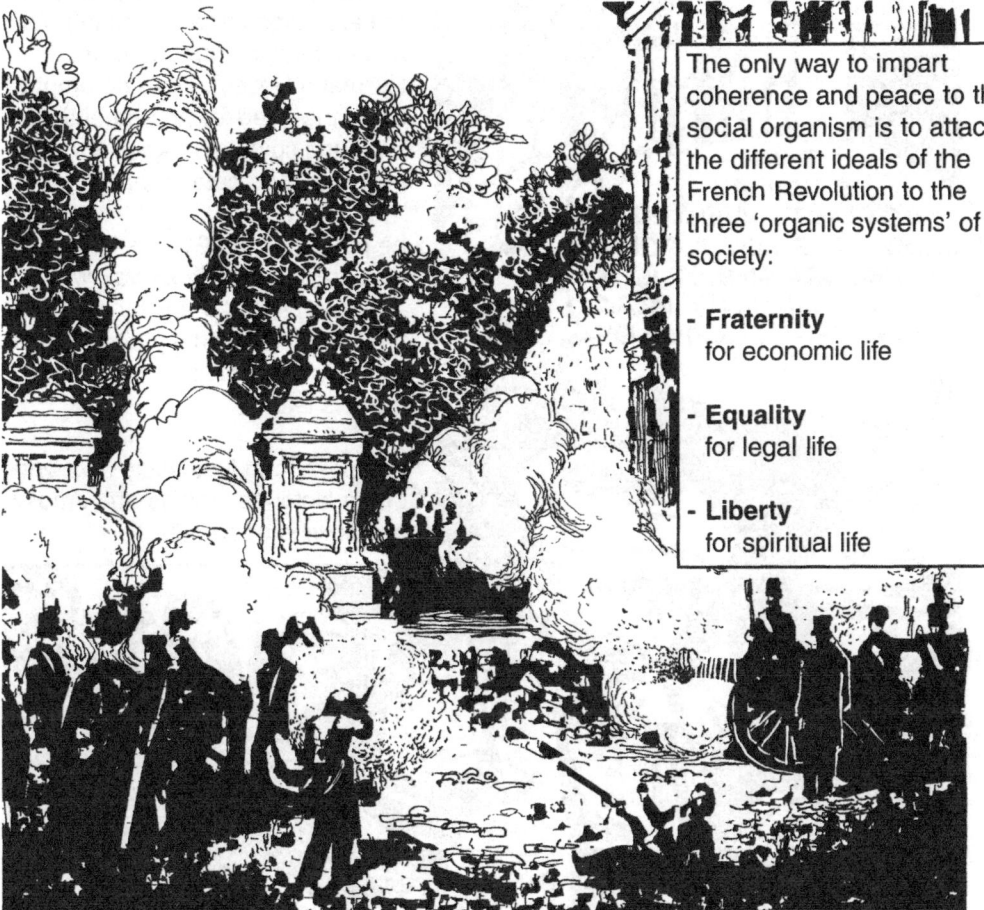

The only way to impart coherence and peace to the social organism is to attach the different ideals of the French Revolution to the three 'organic systems' of society:

- **Fraternity**
  for economic life

- **Equality**
  for legal life

- **Liberty**
  for spiritual life

Only a social organisation conceived in this way could shape authentic democracy, the pure reality of the 'rule of law', social justice and the full development of the human being's creative forces.

During and after the war, Steiner presented his diagnosis and his proposals for a 'cure' for the convulsed society of Europe, in quite diverse environments:

- he met with politicians (ministers, the Austrian Chancellor, etc.);

- he drafted memoranda which were presented to influential persons;

- he gave lectures, as did his associates;

- he published an 'Appeal to the German People and to the World of Culture', signed by a very long list of personages from German public and cultural life (among them Hermann Hesse). Here he emphasised the need for an authentic and profound spiritual renovation 'to prevent future catastrophes';

- he published in 1919 his book **Towards Social Renewal**, which appeared simultaneously in Switzerland, Germany and Austria, with 80,000 copies in print a few months later;

- he spoke to industrialists and workers in factories, unions and smoky, overflowing beer-halls...

THIS IS NOT AN ABSTRACT, INVENTED THEORY, IT IS NOT A POLITICAL PROGRAMME. IT IS A TRUE AND EMINENTLY PRACTICAL UNDERSTANDING OF REALITY!

The working class, shaken by hunger, strikes, armed uprisings, listened to him with hope; he spoke to thousands of workers at the Daimler, Bosch, and Waldorf-Astoria factories, among others. Convinced that the workers' feelings of inferiority were derived not from economic or political limitations, but pre-eminently from cultural ones, he sought to strengthen the dignity of the workers.

"THE INDIVIDUAL'S HUNGER CAN BE SATISFIED BY BREAD; THE COMMUNITY'S HUNGER ONLY BY A CONCEPT OF THE WORLD."

Steiner stated that all human misery comes exclusively from egoism.

"BUT HOW CAN WE OVERCOME EGOISM, IF THE MEASURE OF THE INDIVIDUAL'S WELL-BEING OR MISERY DEPENDS ON HIS CAPACITY FOR WORK?"

The less each person works for himself, and the more he works for others, the better the welfare of a community.

"HUMAN WORK SHOULD NOT BE DEGRADED, LIKE MERCHANDISE TO WHICH WE SET A PRICE. MONEY SERVES TO SATISFY NEEDS, NOT AS COMPENSATION FOR WORK."

> There are many who receive the ideas and approve of them, but very few are willing to really become committed to the ideas and put them into practice.

The intense efforts of Steiner and his followers to implement the tripartite concept of society were hampered by the lack of active participation from other sectors and the opposition of reactionary elements, from both the right and the left.

Even so, the ongoing social movement was the fertile soil in which anthroposophical projects in diverse fields of human activity grew. The most important of these was education.

The Waldorf schools

One of the advocates of social renewal was **Emil Molt**, director of the Waldorf-Astoria cigarette factory in Stuttgart, Germany.

Actively committed to anthroposophy, he was a pioneer in the defence of social welfare. He promoted training and the dignity of the workers, offering them a high-quality internal magazine, a child-care facility, support for their children's education, courses and lectures scheduled during working hours and during the war he even bought a cow so that 'his' children should not go without milk.

These social measures were so unusual at the time, that they earned him an honorary doctorate. He also invited Rudolf Steiner to address his people.

Molt then decided to create a school based on entirely new concepts. He had read a short essay by Steiner written in 1907, 'The Education of the Child in the Light of Anthroposophy'.

CALLED UPON TO DEVELOP AN ART OF EDUCATION, SPIRITUAL SCIENCE WOULD BE ABLE TO INDICATE VERY SPECIFICALLY EVERYTHING NEEDED FOR THIS...

He appealed to Steiner to develop this 'art of education', and Steiner immediately responded with great enthusiasm.

We had neither facilities, nor benches nor books. The school had to emerge from nowhere. But we had in our possession that which was most important: the firm desire to contribute to the progress of humanity and the incalculable good fortune of having Rudolf Steiner as the originator of a new system of education based on his spiritual science.

From his 'more advanced students' Steiner chose twelve people of intermediate age who enthusiastically volunteered to become the first teaching staff. Few of them were already teachers; there were professionals from different areas, artists, artisans... With an intensive course, he prepared them for their new mission.

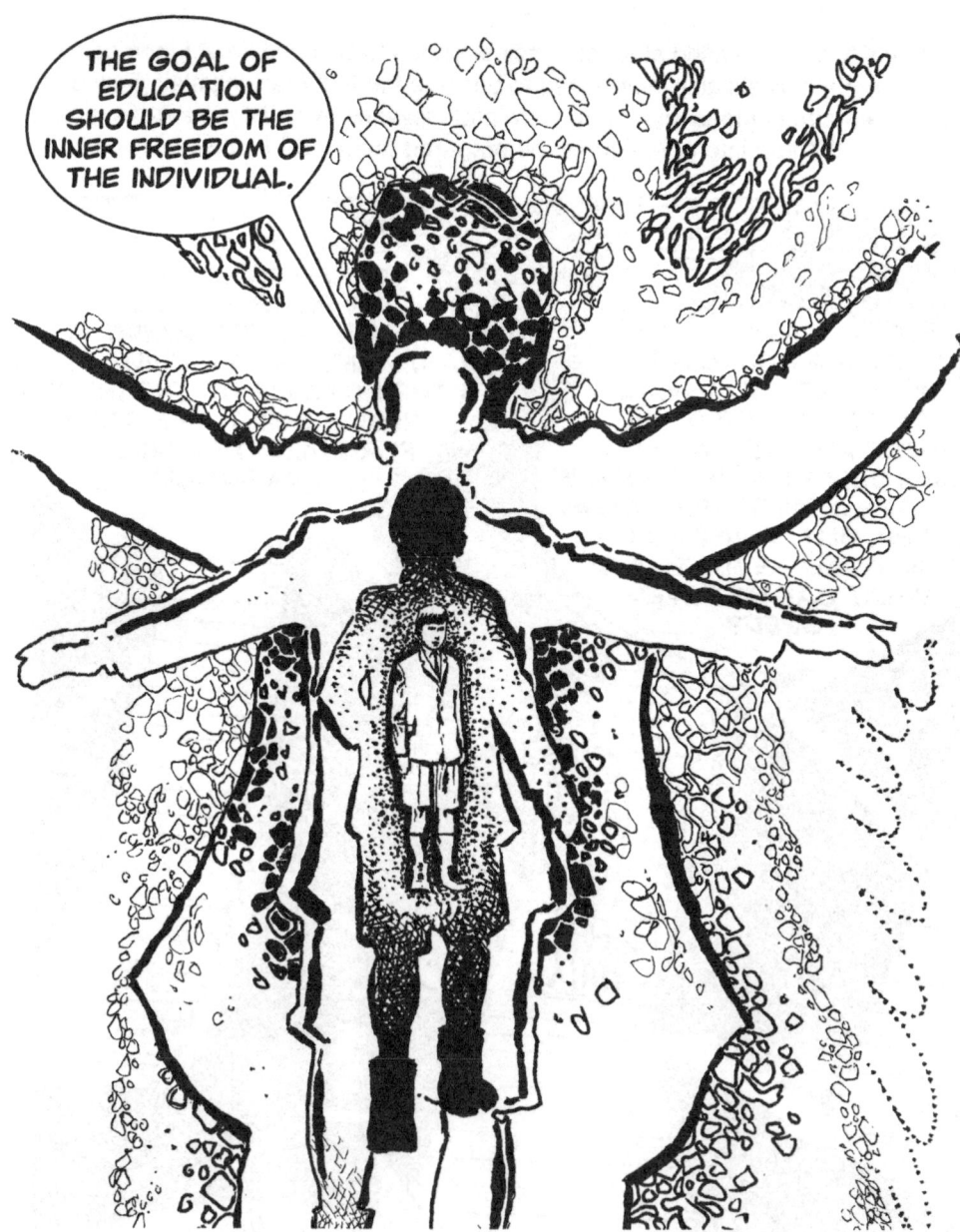

Education should impose no ideology, neither a political, an economic or a religious one—and obviously, not an anthroposophical one either.

Teachers should not teach anthroposophy as a subject, but it should be used for their own training: spiritual science's ideas about the human entity and the 'bodies' of which it is made, about the child's evolutionary stages, about karma and reincarnation, offer the teacher the global image of man which is the basis for the **'Waldorf method'** and the respect for human individuality it requires to carry out its mission with respect and love for the 'self' of each pupil.

If educational effectiveness is to rely more on the personality of the teacher than on any educational programme, then the teacher must always be willing to continue to form his own individuality, to continue to learn from life, from the children.

TO EDUCATE, YOU MUST EDUCATE YOURSELF THROUGHOUT YOUR LIFE. ONLY THE TEACHER WHO IS COMMITTED WILL FIND COMMITTED STUDENTS.

The first group of teachers, encouraged by Rudolf Steiner's warmth, devoted all their energy to this great challenge.

In September 1919, the first Waldorf school opened its doors, with twelve teachers and 256 pupils divided into eight classes. This was the first school in Germany where children of both sexes, different social classes, nationalities and religions all shared a classroom.

A few years later, the school had over 50 teachers and 1,000 students, and was forced to begin rejecting applicants. Meanwhile, families with no connection to the cigarette factory, families from other cities, other countries, that wanted to educate their children according to Steiner's method, also joined the school.

Teachers from other countries, for whom anthroposophy was quite foreign, came as observers of the new method. Rudolf Steiner was invited to speak about it in different European countries, especially in England, a country traditionally interested in education. There he not only met with public recognition, but he became one of the first representatives of German culture who could begin to close the painful gap the war had opened between the two peoples.

Until his death in 1925, Steiner continued to support and guide the Stuttgart school with great dedication: it was his 'favourite child'... In time, this school became the model for the Waldorf movement as it grew internationally. Steiner visited the school frequently, attended lessons and knew every student.

The Waldorf method

The task of the Waldorf teacher is to encourage learning through love and enthusiasm. He must appeal to each student's individuality, 'awakening' him from inside, without indoctrinating him intellectually from outside: to educate him as a human being is more important than to instill knowledge in him.

The school tries, as far as possible, to avoid external coercion: there are no grades in the lower forms, no exams, and no student ever repeats a year. The concept of 'best student' does not exist either: each child's evolution is observed in the context of his own capabilities. At the end of the year, each teacher writes a detailed characterisation of the student in a 'bulletin' that is given to the parents.

The 'homeroom teacher' is responsible for a group of children throughout primary school. Only in this way can the teacher create a real bond and influence each student through his personality, to become—if he succeeds!—the 'beloved authority' that children need at this stage of their development.

The contents of curriculum subjects are conveyed in the so-called 'principal class', which covers the first two hours of the morning, in the form of 'epochs': for some weeks, a subject is studied in a concentrated and intensive way, and then the next one is taken up.

The rest of the daily schedule includes those subjects which require continual exercise: sports, eurythmy, music (all students learn to play the flute and all schools aspire to having choirs and orchestras), etc.

Instruction in the mother tongue and two foreign languages from the first grade—based mainly on storytelling, songs, recitation and staging plays—aims to create a live relation with words and a sensitivity toward other cultures.

The presence of art in the Waldorf schools goes beyond the usual subject matter (which is in any case given considerable time and dedication); art, in addition, confers a creative and aesthetic quality to all the teaching and to the school environment in general.

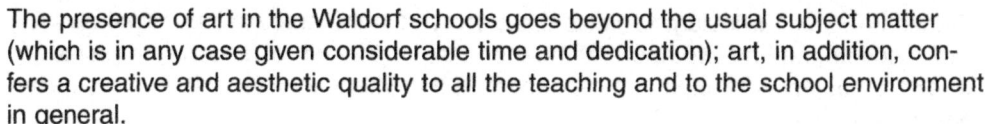

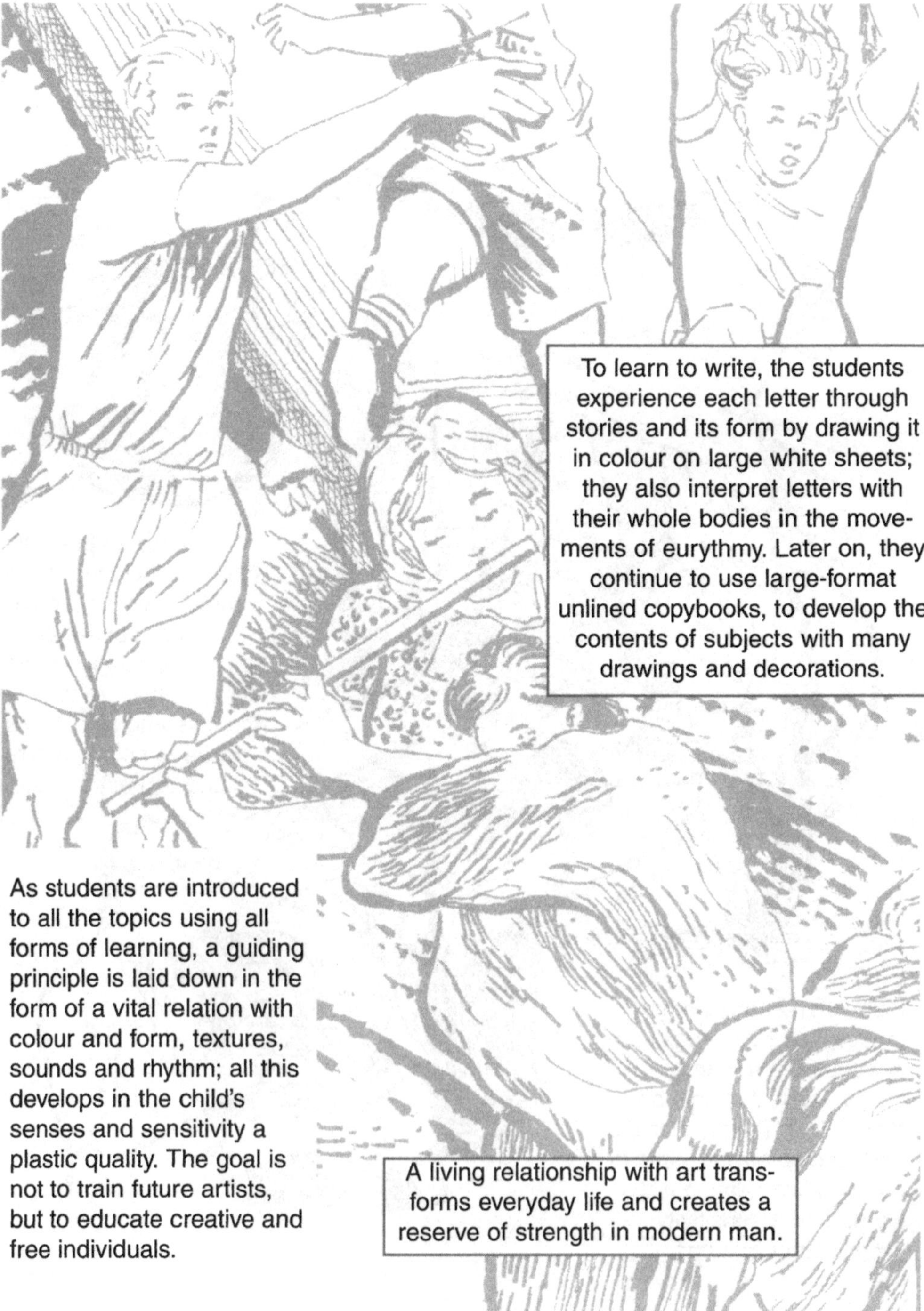

To learn to write, the students experience each letter through stories and its form by drawing it in colour on large white sheets; they also interpret letters with their whole bodies in the movements of eurythmy. Later on, they continue to use large-format unlined copybooks, to develop the contents of subjects with many drawings and decorations.

As students are introduced to all the topics using all forms of learning, a guiding principle is laid down in the form of a vital relation with colour and form, textures, sounds and rhythm; all this develops in the child's senses and sensitivity a plastic quality. The goal is not to train future artists, but to educate creative and free individuals.

A living relationship with art transforms everyday life and creates a reserve of strength in modern man.

Based on the conviction that agility in one's fingers leads to agility in one's thinking, students at the Waldorf schools—girls and boys equally—exercise their manual dexterity through weaving, spinning, knitting, sewing, bookbinding, basket- and paper-making, working with wax, clay, leather, wood, copper, etc.

They also learn to till the soil. In the third grade, they plough and prepare the soil, plant wheat, harvest it by hand, then thresh and mill it and finally make their own bread. In this grade each child also knits a jumper and together they construct a building. The intention is that the children should experience in the archetypal form the tasks that satisfy man's basic needs: providing food, clothing and shelter.

Although Waldorf education is not religious, in the sense of imparting a teaching based on a particular church's conception of the world, Rudolf Steiner saw in the practice of the feeling of veneration, the basis for a religious relationship with the world. That is why Waldorf education seeks to develop devotion toward a divine, deep and responsible respect for nature and human beings.

Waldorf education seeks to nourish not only the intellectual abilities of students, but above all their yearning for creativity and their idealism.

What kind of people does Waldorf education aim to create in order to prepare them for their role in the world?

- **People who have learned to learn, and have learned that a human being has the capacity to become a Man through his entire life.**

- **People who are creative and flexible enough to go beyond pure tradition and conventional knowledge, to be the initiators of cultural progress.**

- **People with a sensitive and open interest in everything that surrounds human beings, in the suffering and joy of their fellows and in everything around us in the world we perceive.**

- **People who trust themselves and who, through experiencing themselves and their social milieu, find a selfhood and a human group which corresponds to their mission in the world.**

- **People who are free inside, exercise social solidarity and are valuable as human beings.**

After Steiner's death in 1925, the Waldorf movement grew quickly: within a few years, schools were established in Germany and also Holland, England, Norway, Switzerland, Portugal, Hungary, and the United States, among others. In 1938, Hitler's regime banned anthroposophical institutions and the German schools had to close. But in 1945, after the war ended, they flourished with increased vigour. In five years, all the old schools were functioning again and twenty new ones had been founded.

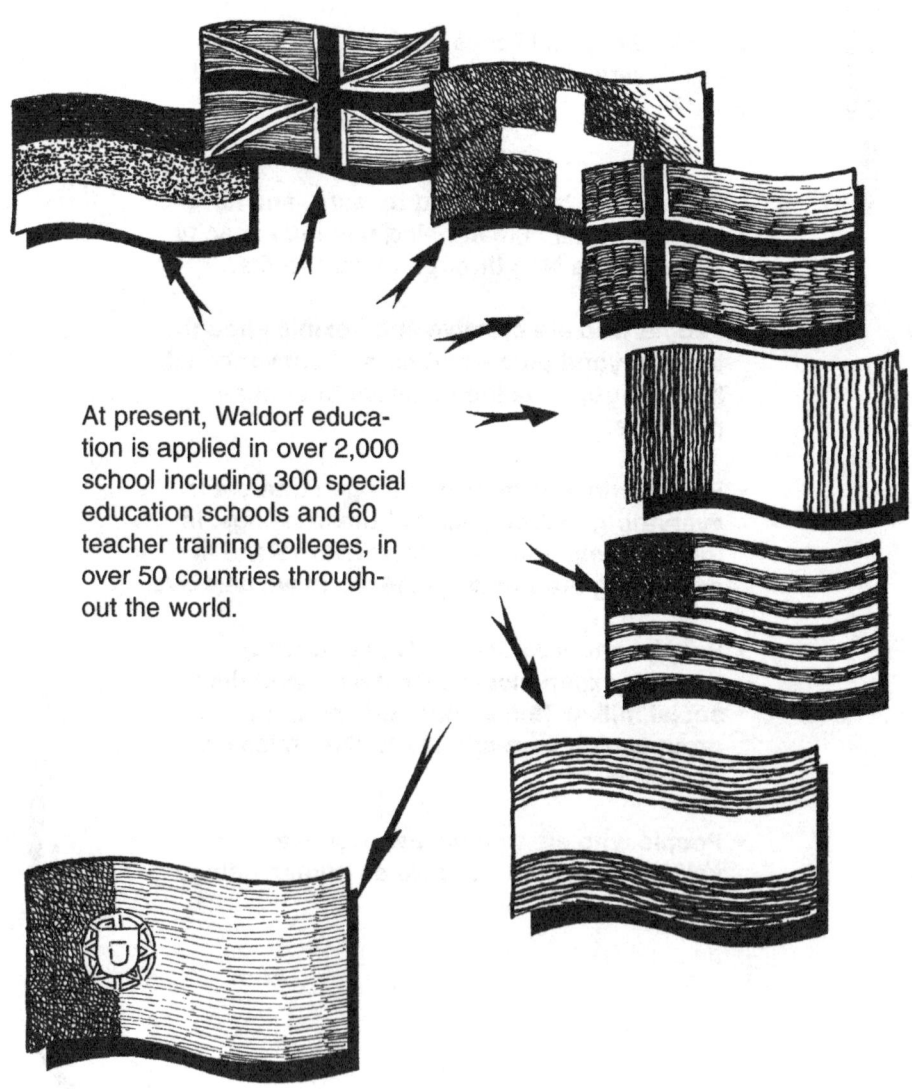

At present, Waldorf education is applied in over 2,000 school including 300 special education schools and 60 teacher training colleges, in over 50 countries throughout the world.

What has not yet been achieved is Steiner's ideal of schools totally independent from the state.

Therapeutic education

Waldorf schools include children with physical and psychological difficulties, providing support for them through special classes, therapeutic eurythmy, etc. For their schoolmates, these children represent one more opportunity to practice solidarity and respect for each human individual.

This kind of education was already offered at the Stuttgart school, under the guidance of Rudolf Steiner, who devised diagnostic criteria and educational and therapeutic measures for children needing in his words, 'special psychological care'.

TO EDUCATE THESE CHILDREN, WHAT IS MOST IMPORTANT IS HUMOUR—REAL HUMOUR, LIVELY HUMOUR!

In anthroposophy, there is no room for the idea of unworthy existences: man's eternal spiritual individuality never gets ill, but sometimes destiny makes it incarnate in a defective bodily instrument; this sets the individual a 'different' life mission, which depends on the love and care of others. The experiences of a life of this sort can be a preparation for another very different, very valuable life.

Once again, it was a concrete request that brought about this new branch of the anthroposophical movement. In 1924, three German students approached Steiner with the aim of creating an institution for the care of children with special needs.

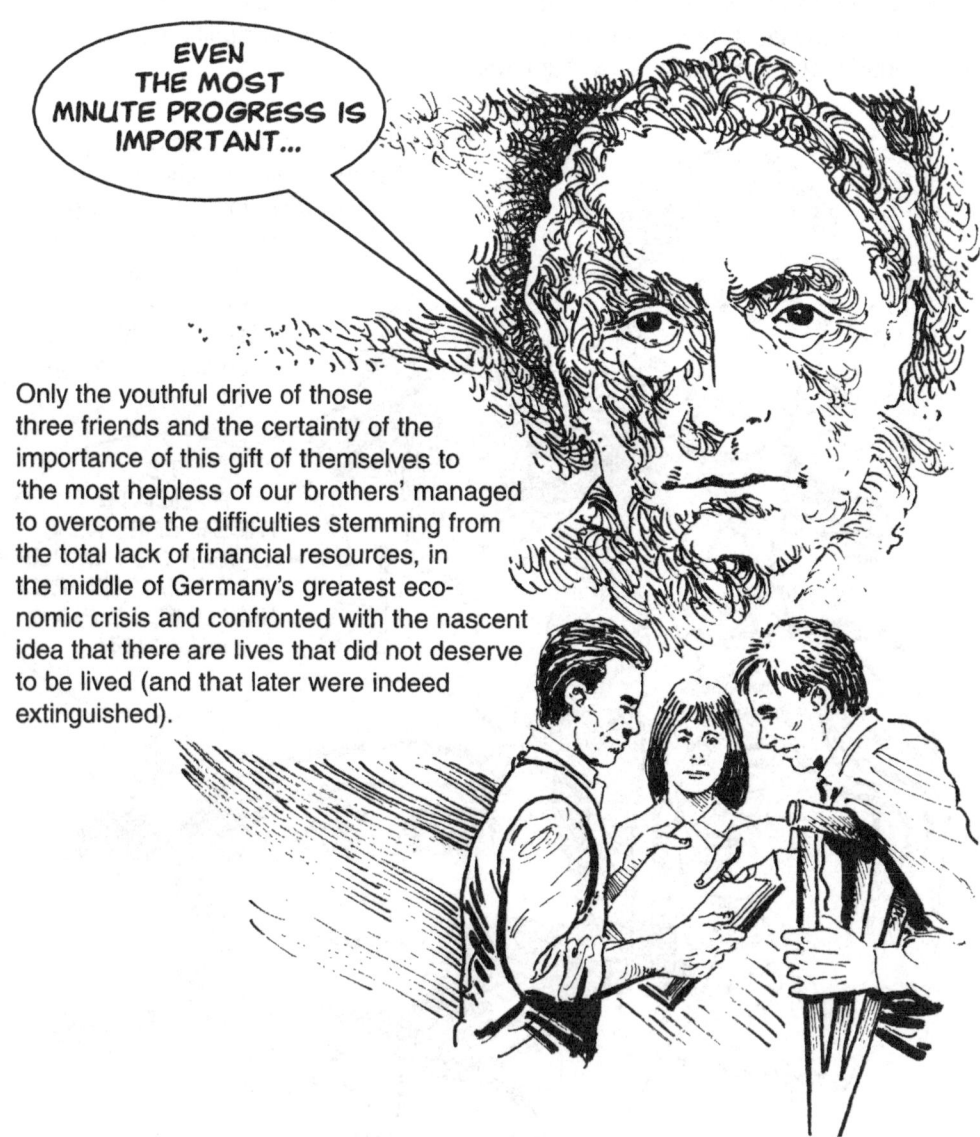

EVEN THE MOST MINUTE PROGRESS IS IMPORTANT...

Only the youthful drive of those three friends and the certainty of the importance of this gift of themselves to 'the most helpless of our brothers' managed to overcome the difficulties stemming from the total lack of financial resources, in the middle of Germany's greatest economic crisis and confronted with the nascent idea that there are lives that did not deserve to be lived (and that later were indeed extinguished).

However, this initiative also managed to expand rapidly: a group of German anthroposophists, exiled from the Third Reich, created the **Camphill movement** in Scotland, consisting of educational therapeutic institutions, and entire villages, where the 'handicapped' lived productively side by side with 'healthy' persons. This model was also adopted in other countries in Europe, and in South Africa and the United States.

An anthroposophical approach to medicine

A different image of the human being also leads, necessarily, to a different approach to disease and healing.

For years, Steiner included themes referring to healthcare in his lectures. Already in 1911, in Prague, he had given a lecture on 'Occult Physiology'.

ONLY THROUGH OBSERVATION OF THE SPIRITUAL IN THE PHYSICAL CAN THE ESSENCE OF THE DISEASE BE RECOGNISED.

In 1917, in his book *Metamorphoses of the Soul*, he explained his vision of the human organism's functions, in close inter-relation with psychological life.

Contrary to the traditional concept, which assigned all psychological activity to processes of the nervous system, for Steiner three functional systems existed, each of which had its own dynamics and carried one of the three fundamental psychological activities.

- The neuro-sensory system (brain, senses), located principally in the head, the bearer of 'thinking'.

- The metabolic-motor system (digestion, extremities), located in the abdomen and the members, the bearer of 'will'.

These two systems have dynamics which are polar opposites: the first is characterised by quietude, cold, 'death' (catabolic processes); the second by movement, heat, vitality (anabolic processes). As mediator between both extremes there is:.

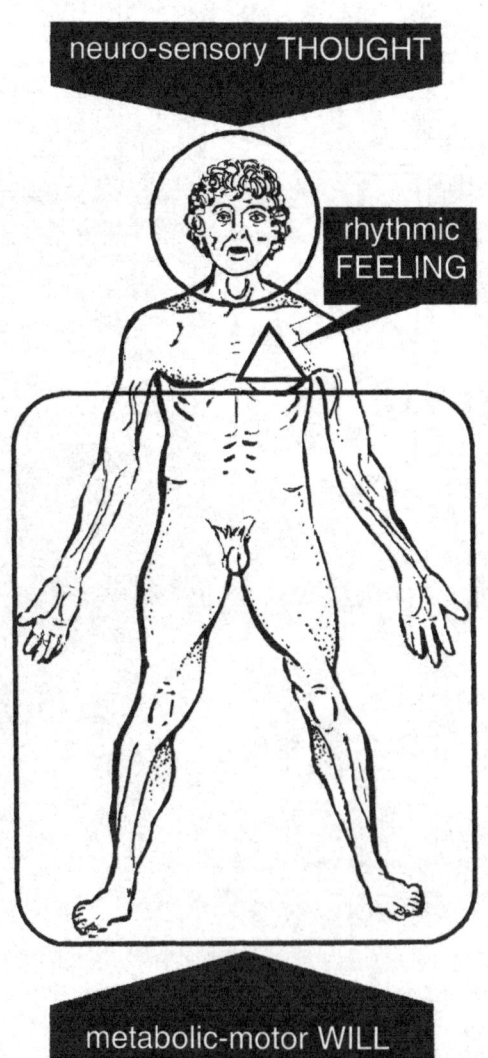

- The rhythmic system (breathing, blood circulation) located around the heart, the carrier of 'feeling'. In permanent oscillation between the two extremes, it must harmonise them. The resultant equilibrium—health—is not static; it depends, among other factors, on age: at the beginning of life the inferior pole's strength (vitality) is necessarily dominant; at the end of life, the higher pole (quietude) is dominant.

The organism's basic pathological tendencies manifest when there is an overflow (the untimely and out of place presence) of one of the two dynamics: if the neuro-sensory pole predominates, there will be hardening, deposits, premature ageing (sclerotic, rheumatic, arthritic diseases); if the metabolic-motor pole predominates, inflammatory diseases will appear (fevers, infections).

The drive for a renewal of medicine based on anthroposophy began, however, only in 1920, when at a public lecture a pharmacologist asked Steiner to provide a course for health professionals.

In the following years he gave several lecture series for doctors and medical students, demonstrating surprising mastery in this subject too.

WHAT YOU ARE SEARCHING FOR IS THE HUMANISATION OF MEDICINE!

Ita Wegman (1876-1943)

The Dutch doctor **Ita Wegman** established near the Goetheanum, a clinic where Steiner's innumerable suggestions began to be applied. At any hour of the day or night, he was willing to come and help the doctors, analyse actual cases, explain his criteria, diagnose and suggest treatment. However, he never acted therapeutically on his own (and even less so in any 'magical' way): all his instructions—anybody can reproduce them—were intended for doctors who were interested in developing 'medicine with an anthroposophical orientation'.

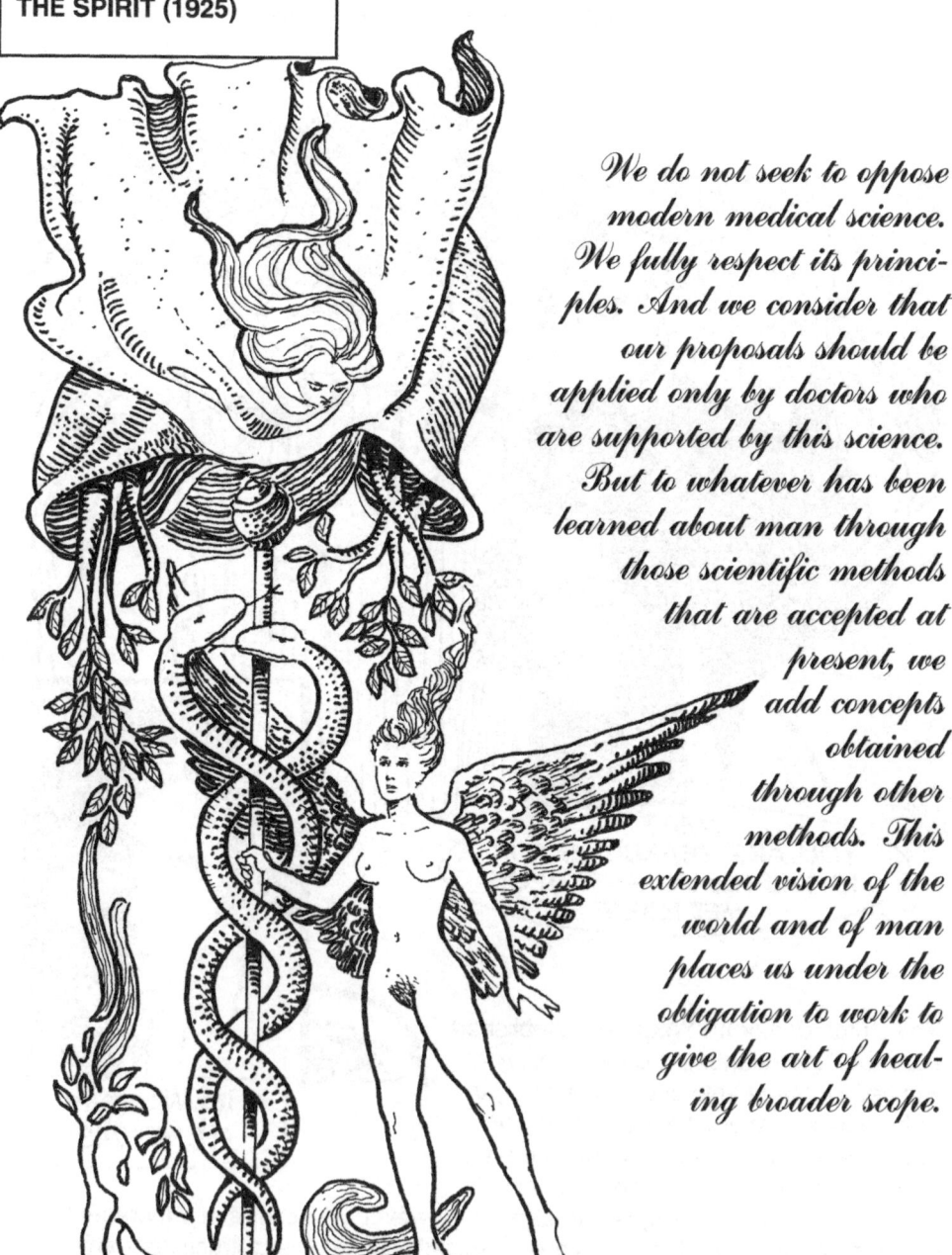

EXTENDING PRACTICAL MEDICINE: FUNDAMENTAL PRINCIPLES BASED ON THE SCIENCE OF THE SPIRIT (1925)

Steiner's book, written with Ita Wegman, and published posthumously is a treatise on anthroposophical medicine.

We do not seek to oppose modern medical science. We fully respect its principles. And we consider that our proposals should be applied only by doctors who are supported by this science. But to whatever has been learned about man through those scientific methods that are accepted at present, we add concepts obtained through other methods. This extended vision of the world and of man places us under the obligation to work to give the art of healing broader scope.

This 'extended vision' of the human being, consisting of body, soul and spirit, can hardly look upon health and disease only as good or bad 'functioning' at the physical level. A conception of life according to which each human individual is led by destiny along a path where he achieves perfection through a succession of incarnations on earth, would refuse to see in disease something which 'attacks' the organism from outside, for physical and chemical reasons foreign to it.

THE POSSIBILITY OF BECOMING SICK GUARANTEES THAT YOU ARE AUTHENTICALLY HUMAN. IT IS THE TOOL FOR OVERCOMING OBSTACLES IN EVOLUTION WHICH HAD, OTHERWISE, BEEN IMPOSSIBLE TO OVERCOME.

In this sense, healing will also not be content with eliminating the symptoms quickly (the more efficient the substances the pharmaceutical industry provides, the greater is the temptation to do this). It will not be enough for healing to correct observable physical alterations and normalise laboratory values, eliminate 'discomfort' and suffering and give back to the individual his capacity to work.

Anthroposophical medicine is not content to 'cure' diseases; instead, it seeks to 'heal' the sick person.

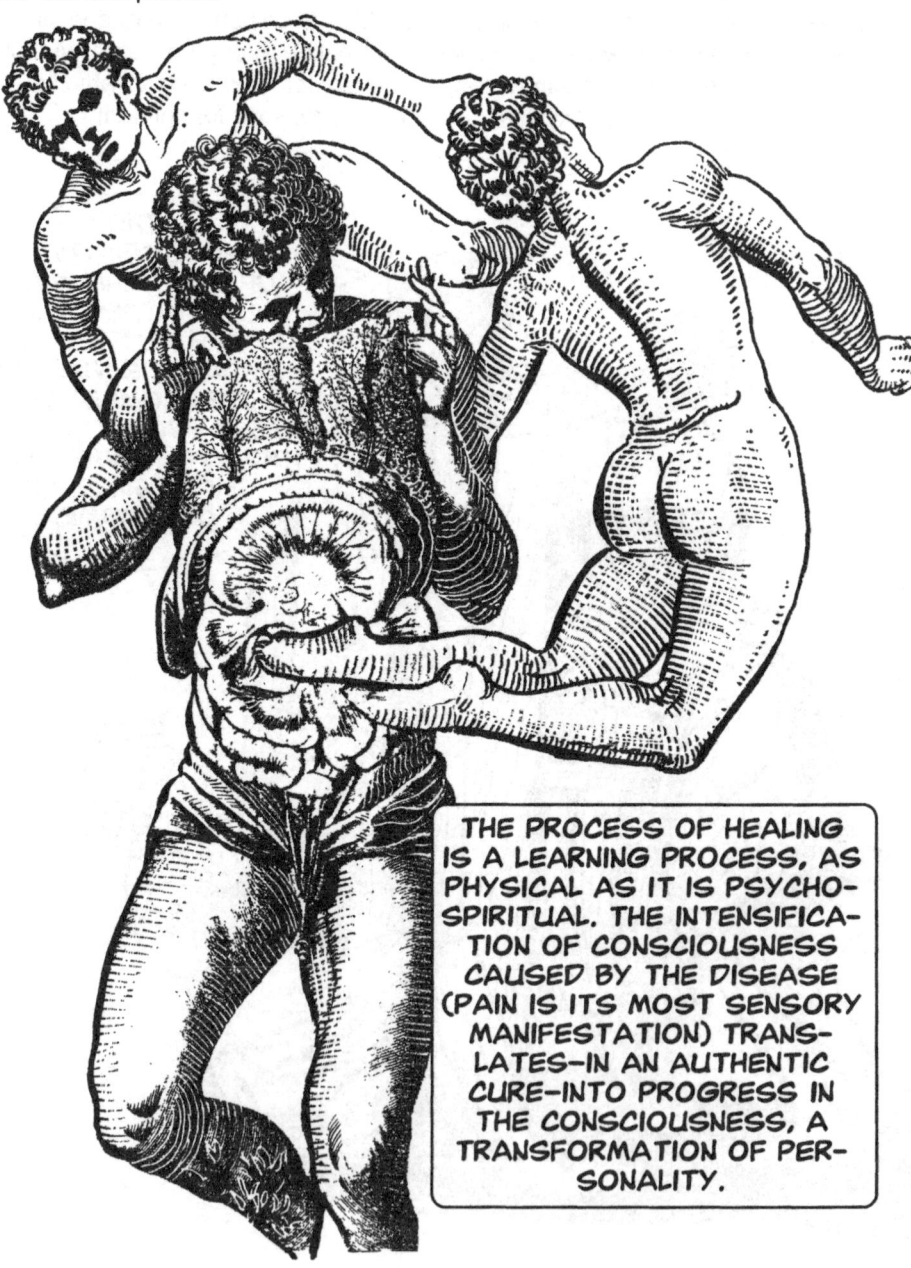

THE PROCESS OF HEALING IS A LEARNING PROCESS, AS PHYSICAL AS IT IS PSYCHO-SPIRITUAL. THE INTENSIFICATION OF CONSCIOUSNESS CAUSED BY THE DISEASE (PAIN IS ITS MOST SENSORY MANIFESTATION) TRANSLATES—IN AN AUTHENTIC CURE—INTO PROGRESS IN THE CONSCIOUSNESS, A TRANSFORMATION OF PERSONALITY.

The job for the anthroposophically-minded doctor is to determine the source of the patient's evolutionary path and where it is going (in an integral sense: physical, psychological and spiritual) and to support and guide this process (also in an integral sense).

For those doctors who chose to be his students, Rudolf Steiner represented the ideal of the 'art of healing' that they aspired to approach through the long and laborious training of the corresponding 'organs of perception':

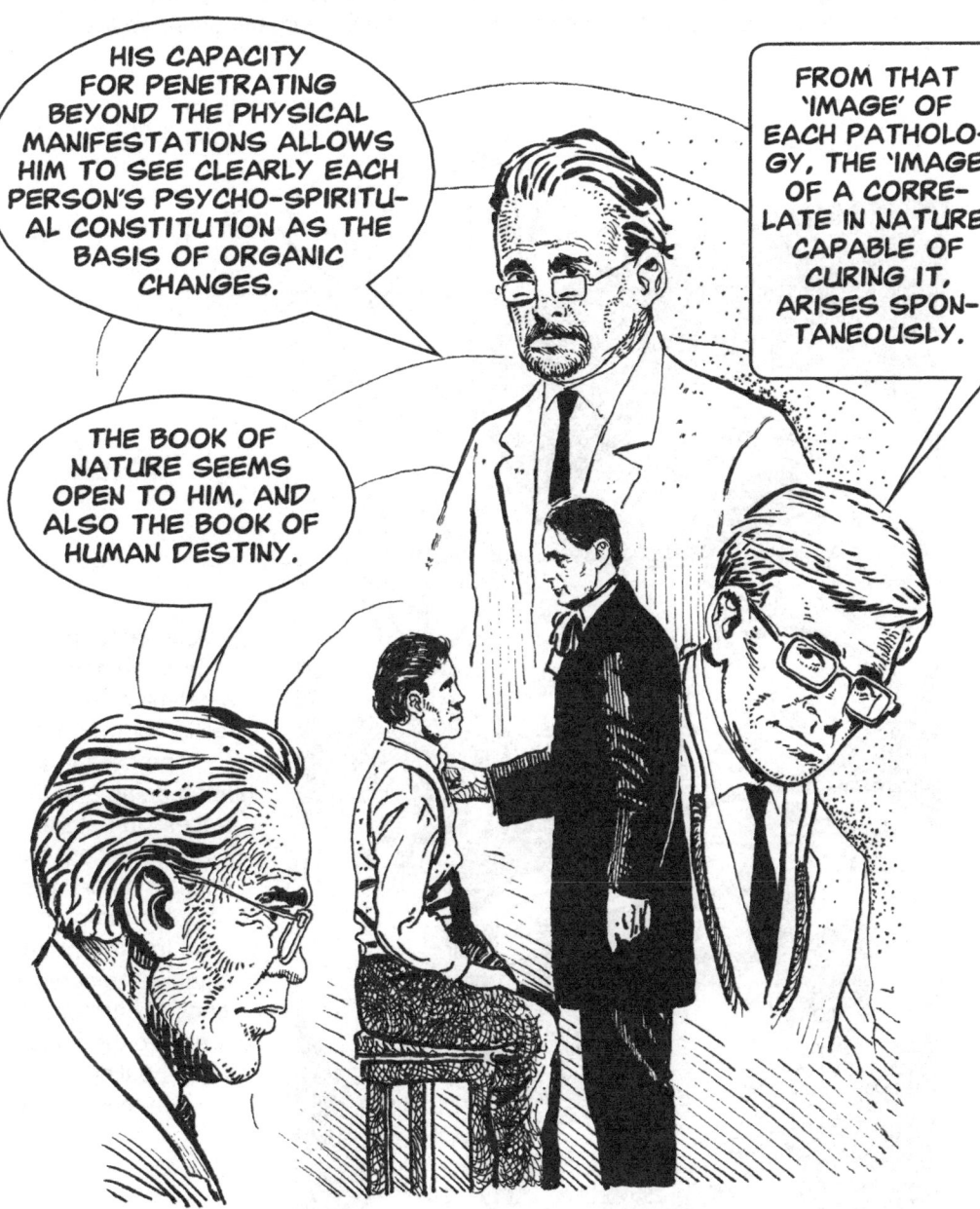

In Steiner and Wegman's book, a series of patients' histories serve as examples of the anthroposophical concept of disease: each of them describes the real and specific incidence of the etheric body, the astral body and the self in the corresponding pathology.

According to Steiner's cosmogony, the beings and processes of nature which surround man are what he has left behind in his evolutionary process on earth.

To each organic process in the human being there corresponds a process in nature. These have separated at some moment of evolution, but preserve their intrinsic affinity.

Anthroposophical medicine seeks to re-establish the connection between the process in the human being and the process in nature. It gives the patient the process 'model' that can guide the organism toward the re-establishment of its original harmony. It appeals to the forces of self-healing in the human being.

Anthroposophical medicines come from the three realms of nature.

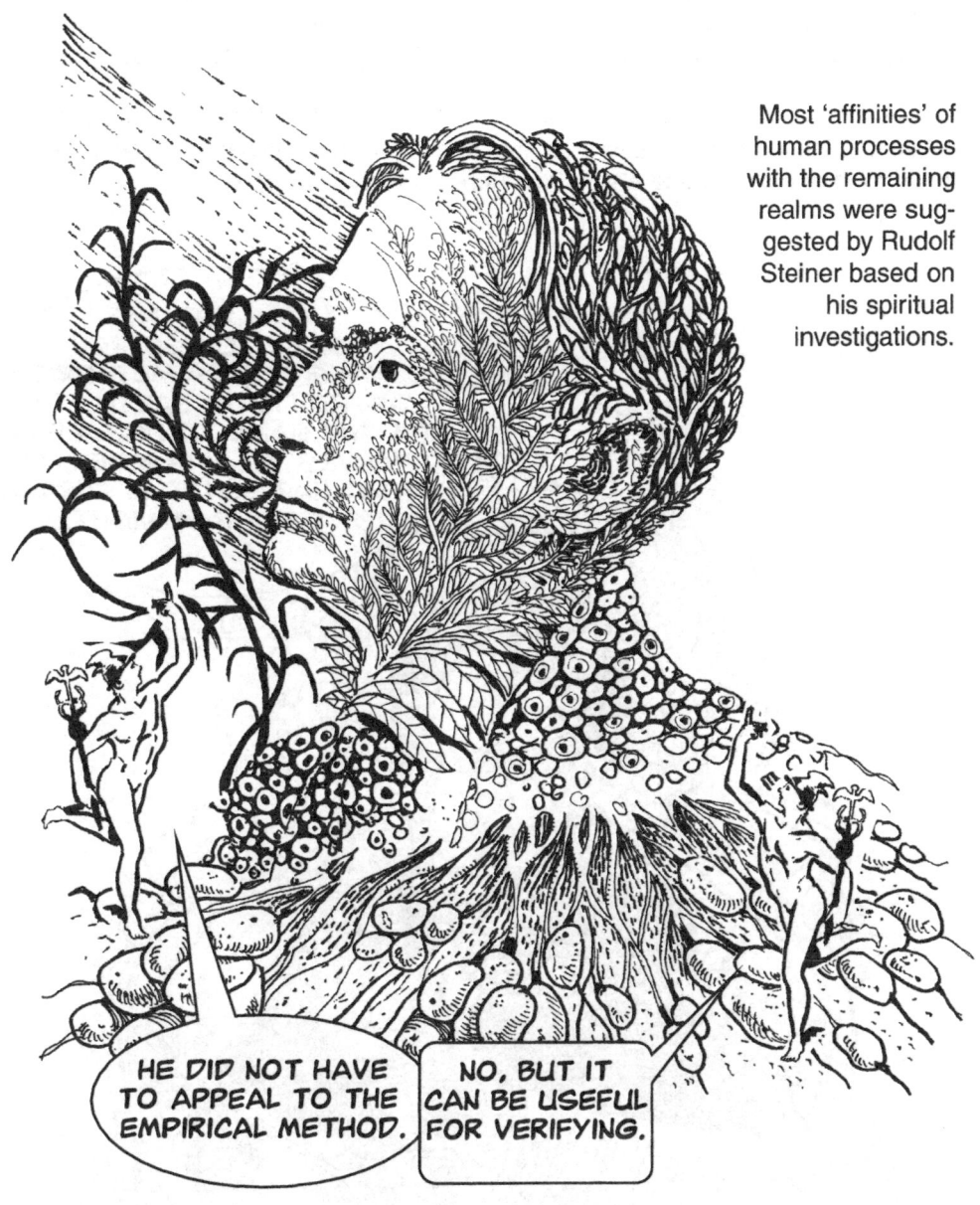

Most 'affinities' of human processes with the remaining realms were suggested by Rudolf Steiner based on his spiritual investigations.

HE DID NOT HAVE TO APPEAL TO THE EMPIRICAL METHOD.

NO, BUT IT CAN BE USEFUL FOR VERIFYING.

The earliest medicines were developed in the small laboratory created in the Goetheanum for preparing pigments for the frescoes of the cupolas. Soon the Weleda company was founded for the development and production of special medicines using the criteria of spiritual science.

The anthroposophical pharmacopoeia is not based on the effect of a so-called 'active substance', isolated from the natural (vital) context or even manufactured synthetically in a laboratory. Instead, it seeks to 'tap' in each medicine a particular process, the complex interaction of forces which originated the substance.

Because of the importance attributed to the dynamics of each substance, account is taken of the medium it came from, the moment it was obtained and especially the form of processing and also administering it to the sick person.

Among the methods for preparing medicines, making substances more potent and dynamic plays a leading role. This procedure was discovered empirically by **Samuel Hahnemann**, the creator of **homeopathy**.

It involves a number of rhythmic steps, taken to dilute (or grind) the substance in a 'vehicle'.

Anthroposophical medicine took this method of preparation from homeopathy, just as it draws from other sources or confirms from knowledge acquired through its own methods, discoveries obtained through the traditional intuitive method (natural medicine) or the modern scientific one ('allopathic' medicine).

Basically, as many as 30 decimal dilutions (D1 to D30) are used. The higher the potency, more present is the 'dynamic' of the substance. As it disappears physically (in the D1 to D10 range, the presence of molecules from the 'mother' substance can still be detected, but then they disappear progressively) there is an increase in the etheric and astral effectiveness incorporated in the 'vehicle'.

Anthroposophical medicines consist of minerals (among these, metals are especially relevant), and substances having vegetable and animal origin. There are also compound medicines, the contents of which were, for the most, part recommended by Steiner.

AS A SCIENTIST, I FEEL COMPELLED TO REJECT THIS PROCEDURE: IF THERE IS NO PROVABLE SUBSTANCE, THERE CAN BE NO EFFECT!

MATERIALIST!

According to the therapeutic concept based on anthroposophy, it is the patient himself who is truly responsible for the cure: he is not a 'patient' (the passive object of the 'treatment' imposed by the doctor), but the active subject of his own health.

In this sense, the practice of some artistic activity is recommended, as well as specific exercises of therapeutic eurythmy. Of greatest importance, however, is work on the person's self, the evolution of consciousness.

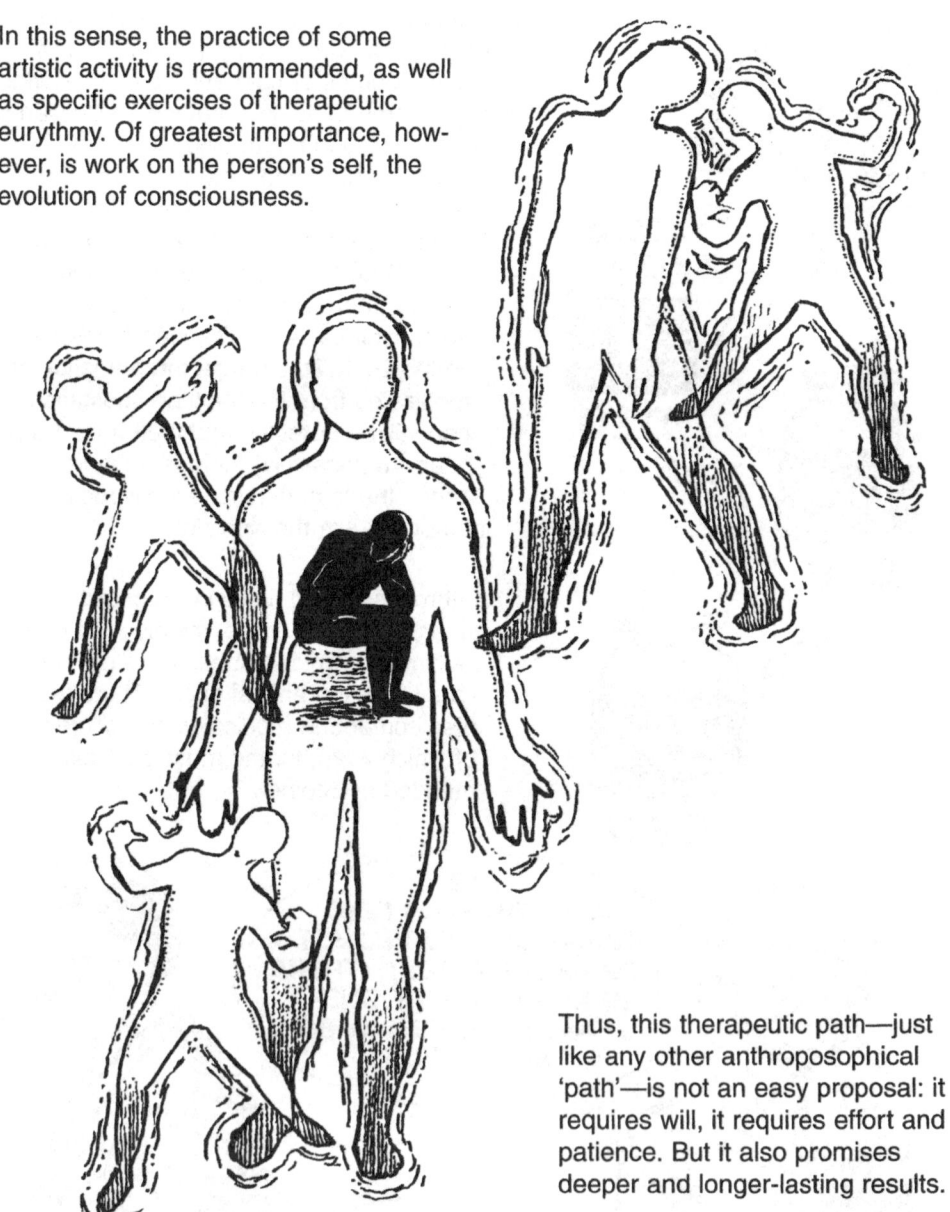

Thus, this therapeutic path—just like any other anthroposophical 'path'—is not an easy proposal: it requires will, it requires effort and patience. But it also promises deeper and longer-lasting results.

Bio-dynamic agriculture

Among Steiner's followers, there were also farmers who asked for his guidance.

Interested persons from different professions who came looking for the wisdom of the great master and initiate, were always astounded when he exhibited detailed and practical mastery of their speciality. He continued to emphasise that all the erudition in the world is good for nothing if it does not continuously relate to the practical aspects of life.

Steiner then discussed the processes (here too the dynamics of life were more relevant than the chemistry of inert substances) which act through earth, water, light and the sun's heat. He gave very specific 'prescriptions' for appropriate products and processes for the sanitation of the soil, vegetables and animals—and with this also human beings—several decades before the birth of 'ecological awareness'. The suggestions that that first circle of enthusiasts received, became in time 'bio-dynamic agriculture', which produces food products in many countries of the world, taking special care of their biological quality.

The Community of Christians

In three courses on theoretical and practical theology, Steiner again surprised specialists in the field with his specific knowledge. At the request of future clergymen, he discussed the bases and needs of a religious life consistent with contemporary lifestyles. He suggested rituals to renew the Christian sacraments.

In 1923, the **Community of Christians** was created under the leadership of the Protestant clergyman **Dr Friedrich Rittelmeyer** who was quite well-known in the German Lutheran church. His sermons attracted large crowds. He approached anthroposophy with caution, but also with great conviction and enthusiasm and finally joined the movement. In his book, *My Life Encounter with Rudolph Steiner*, he described this process vividly. The Community of Christians was characterised by the freedom that reigned within it: it was not based on dogmas, it imposed no beliefs. There, for the first time, were women acting as priests. While this was a form of Christianity based on Steiner's thought, he declared that the Community of Christians and the Anthroposophical Society were quite distinct and separate organisations.

> *The search for scientific truths about the spiritual world has nothing to do with religion But a properly understood anthroposophy will also create a real and authentic religious need. For human souls need different paths to advance to their goal. But anthroposophy interferes with no-one's creed.*

Along with his 'academic courses', Steiner continued to give talks in many European cities, for anthroposophists and also for the general public. He never sought publicity for his activities, his books and even less his ideas.

HE WHO WISHES TO HEAR, LET HIM HEAR!

But more and more people *did* want to listen to him. His tours became dramatic.

On 26 January 1922 he spoke at the Philharmonic in Berlin. The police were forced to maintain order among the thousands who jostled to gain admittance.

The most notable anthroposophical event in Steiner's life was the East-West Congress. For twelve days in June 1922, 2,000 enthusiasts of anthroposophy from all over the world filled the lecture rooms and theatres of Vienna to hear lectures, seminars and public discussions on the most diverse scientific topics, and to attend artistic evenings. At the hotel where Steiner stayed, hundreds of people waited night and day for a personal interview with the master.

There, in the heart of Europe, Steiner tried to make people aware of antagonisms between East and West that would only explode decades later.

However, lights project shadows. Steiner's philosophy of freedom and spirituality seemed to especially preoccupy the most hardened members of ecclesiastical and nationalist circles.

> THE FATHERLAND IS A CULTURAL ENTITY. PATRIOTISM IS JUSTIFIED ONLY AT THE CULTURAL LEVEL. IF THE THREEFOLD ORGANISATION WERE APPLIED, NATIONAL BORDERS WOULD GRADUALLY DISAPPEAR.

> POLITICS IS WAR AND PREPARING FOR WAR. FOR EACH PEOPLE WANTS TO DOMINATE THE WORLD.

This led to attacks, which the press printed. The lectures in Germany were disturbed by rallies and insults, threats of arson and bombs. Personal aggression against Steiner forced his followers to organise to protect the master and the centre in Dormach. Imperturbably, Rudolf Steiner continued on his path, disdaining discussions or clashes.

During the Third Reich, the attacks would culminate in the confiscation of all Steiner's books. Anthroposophical organisations were forbidden, their property expropriated, farmers, teachers and clergymen incarcerated.
However, efforts to maintain anthroposophical activities received unexpected help. **Rudolf Hess**, the high-ranking Nazi, worked hard in his garden, but it languished, while his neighbour's prospered magnificently. Hess studied the subject, obtained good results, and from then on Steiner's followers had a protector, until Hess decide to parachute over England!

> HOW DID HE DO IT?

> USING THE BIO-DYNAMIC SYSTEM.

The Goetheanum fire

On 31 December 1922, while Rudolf Steiner was ending the year at the Goetheanum with a talk on 'Humanity's Spiritual Communion', anonymous hands set fire to the double wooden wall. A witness described the scene:

JUST AFTER TEN AT NIGHT, WHEN THE LAST VISITORS HAD LEFT THE ROOM, THE WATCHMAN ON DUTY SAW SMOKE. THE ENTIRE TEAM OF VOLUNTEERS WAS IMMEDIATELY MOBILISED. FIREMEN, SUPPORTED BY HUNDREDS OF HELPERS WHO STREAMED IN FROM NEARBY, RECKLESSLY RISKED THEIR LIVES. INSIDE, THE ROAR OF THE FLAMES GREETED US. WE SAVED WHATEVER COULD BE CARRIED, BUT SOON THE SMOKE WAS SO DENSE THAT IT BECAME IMPOSSIBLE TO BREATHE. RUDOLF STEINER ORDERED EVERYBODY OUT OF THE BUILDING... IT WAS ONLY LEFT TO US TO PROTECT THE NEIGHBOURING BUILDINGS, THE CARPENTRY SHOP AND THE WORKSHOP WITH THE GREAT STATUE, STILL UNFINISHED. AT MIDNIGHT WHEN BELLS RANG IN THE NEW YEAR, THE CUPOLAS CRASHED DOWN. GREEN AND BLUE FLAMES LEAPED FROM THE ORGAN'S METALLIC PIPES. LIKE AN ENORMOUS TORCH, THE GOETHEANUM BURNED, AN UNFORGETTABLE SIGHT, FILLED WITH HORROR AND BEAUTY. RUDOLF STEINER STOOD WATCHING UNTIL MORNING. NO TRACE OF RANCOUR MARRED HIS DEEP GAZE, ONLY IMMEASURABLE PAIN AND GRIEF.

1 January 1923

"WE WILL GO ON WITH THE LECTURE AND THE PLAY SCHEDULED FOR TODAY. PREPARE THE CARPENTRY SHOP."

Long before the scheduled time, the carpentry shop was packed. Hundreds of people waited in silence. When Steiner entered, they stood in mute and affectionate solidarity.

"WHAT CAN I SAY ABOUT OUR GOETHEANUM? WITH LOVE WE BUILT IT. WITH LOVE WE WORKED IN IT. WITH LOVE WE HAVE SEEN IT DISAPPEAR. NOW WE WILL CONTINUE OUR WORK."

He then went on, serene and concentrated, to speak of 'The Origins of Natural Science'.

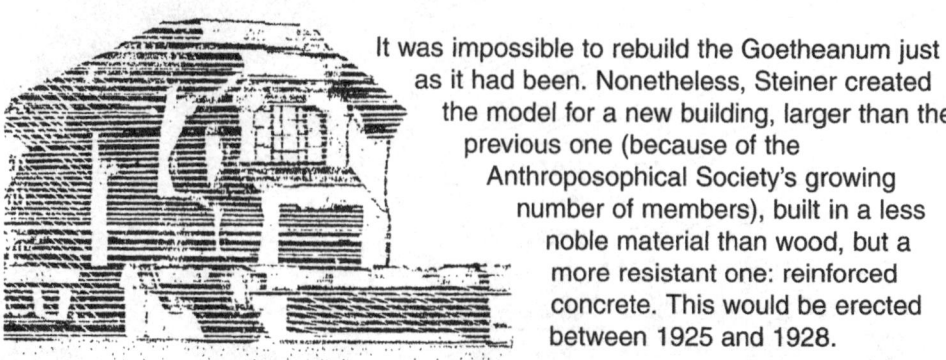

It was impossible to rebuild the Goetheanum just as it had been. Nonetheless, Steiner created the model for a new building, larger than the previous one (because of the Anthroposophical Society's growing number of members), built in a less noble material than wood, but a more resistant one: reinforced concrete. This would be erected between 1925 and 1928.

1924 to 1925

Far from becoming engulfed in accusation and persecution, Steiner sought to prevail over this 'trial by fire' for the anthroposophical movement, by strengthening it from within. He intensified his activity even further: he travelled more, gave more courses and talks (usually four a day), took care of the school, the clinic, began work on the new Goetheanum, kept up a huge correspondence and received hundreds of people who came every day to obtain his advice. At night, when the others had fallen into exhausted sleep, he wrote.

NOW PERHAPS LESS WILL BE SAID ABOUT FRATERNITY, LESS ABOUT LOVE FOR HUMANITY, BUT THESE FEELINGS WILL BE ALIVE IN PEOPLE'S HEARTS.

It was as if he wanted to give form again to everything he had created, and leave it finished, for the time when he would no longer be there. The greater affluence of new members and the creation of new anthroposophical institutions had diverted the movement's initial path, and blurred its purpose. It was now necessary to redefine its goals. Steiner re-founded the Anthroposophical Society, insisting once again on the need to keep it free from all kinds of dogmatism and sectarianism, from conventionalism and routine, from mysticism, grandiloquence and concealment. He demanded absolute realism, absolute authenticity.

In January 1924, Steiner began to suffer from a gastric disorder that was so severe that he was barely able to eat (some suspected that it came from an attempt to poison him). To the consternation of all those who loved and admired him, he did not slow down, and continued to carry his superhuman burden of work (never in his life did he cancel a lecture). Neither did he lose his serene and affable disposition or his quite personal sense of humour.

By September, he could no longer stand. His sickbed was set up in his 'atelier', at the foot of the unfinished statue of Christ. From there, he continued to stay in touch with his people through letters, articles and books. At the insistent request of his students, he began to write his autobiography in which, besides describing his own evolution in great detail, he painted a colourful fresco of the cultural life of the time. Each week, he sent a chapter to the printer, with a note saying 'to be continued'. In the last week of March 1925—the story had reached the turn of the century—the manuscript no longer bore that note.

On 30 March 1925, Rudolph Steiner died.

Many among those who knew him felt the historic obligation to give an account of their 'life encounter' with Rudolf Steiner, and of their gratitude and admiration for the master's life.

HE WAS A PORTENTOUSLY GREAT SAGE, YET HE WAS EVEN GREATER AS A HUMAN BEING. (H. HAHN)

WHOEVER WOULD LIKE TO UNDERSTAND WHAT THAT DEATH MEANT TO US, MUST UNDERSTAND WHAT THAT LIFE MEANT TO US. (F. POEPPIG)

THE GENEROSITY AND ABSOLUTE RESPECT FOR HUMAN DIGNITY WITH WHICH HE USED TO HEAR OUT EVERY PERSON CALLED FORTH DEEP TRUST AND TRUST IN ONE'S SELF. (H. HAHN)

YOU FELT THAT HE KNEW YOU, KNEW YOU IN THE DEPTH OF YOUR TEMPORAL AND ETERNAL BEING, KNEW YOUR DESTINY—THE GOOD AND THE EVIL OF IT—FROM THE WARMTH WITH WHICH HE RECEIVED YOU AND HELD OUT HIS HAND TO LEAD YOU TO YOURSELF. (A. TURGENIEFF)

I FELT FREER THAN EVER, AS IF ADMITTED TO ANOTHER WORLD WHERE ONLY WHAT IS ESSENTIAL COUNTS. (F.W. ZEYLMANS VAN EMMICHOVEN))

Even his mother-in-law used to remark: 'His wisdom, his influence and renown have no importance for me: but his immense goodness does'.

Neither the fervent admiration of his followers nor the inflamed contempt of his opponents have prevented Rudolf Steiner, in the hundred years that have gone by, from remaining virtually unknown to the 'official culture' of the entire world.

• It is true that it is very hard to 'prove' everything he affirmed...

• It is true that his work is overwhelmingly vast, hermetic, and mentions entities which cannot be seen, or touched, or measured, in a personal, obscure language, with a whiff of mysticism...

• It is true that his followers have not always been able to avoid instances of meanness and arrogance, messianism and sectarianism...

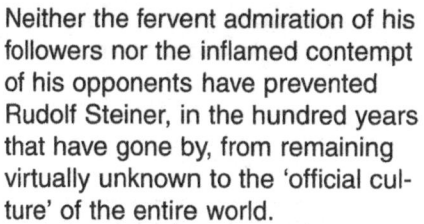

Anthroposophical organisations

Australia
Anthroposophical Society, Sydney Branch
307 Sussex St
Sydney

Canada
Anthroposophical Society in Canada/ Société
    Anthroposophique au Canada
PO Box 38162
550 Eglinton Avenue West
Toronto
Ontario M5N 3A8

Great Britain
Anthroposophical Society in Great Britain
Rudolf Steiner House
35 Park Road
London NW1 6XT

New Zealand
Anthroposophical Society of New Zealand
RD2
Hastings

Switzerland
General Anthroposophical Society
PO Box CH-4143
Dormach 1

United States
Anthroposophical Society in America
Ann Arbor
MICHIGAN 48104-1797

Bibliography

Steiner's Main Works

Anthroposophy in Everyday Life, Anthroposophic Press, 1995
Autobiography: Chapters in the Course of My Life, 1861-1907,
   Anthroposophic Press, 1999
Christianity As Mystical Fact, Anthroposophic Press, 1997
The Education of the Child in the Light of Anthroposophy, O/P
Extending Practical Medicine, Garber Communications, 1998
Friedrich Nietzsche: Fighter for Freedom, Lindisfarne Books, 1985
Goethe's Conception of the World, O/P
How to Know Higher Worlds, Anthroposophic Press, 1994
Intuitive Thinking as a Spiritual Path, Anthroposophic Press, 1995
Metamorphoses of the Soul, Anthroposophic Press, 1983
Mysticism at the Dawn of the Modern Age, Garber Communications, 1980
An Outline of Occult Science, Kessinger Publishing Co, 1998
Philosophy of Freedom, O/P
*Theosophy: An Introduction to the Spiritual Process in Human Life and in
   the Cosmos*, Anthroposophic Press, 1994
Towards Social Renewal (1919), O/P
A Way to Self-Knowledge, Anthroposophic Press, 1999

Books about Rudolf Steiner/Anthroposophy

Barnes, Henry (ed)	*A Life for the Spirit: Rudolf Steiner in the Crosscurrents of Our Time* Anthroposophic Press, 1997
Childs, Gilbert	*Steiner Education in Theory and Practice* Anthroposophic Press, 1994
Easton, Stewart C.	*Rudolf Steiner: Herald of a New Epoch* Anthroposophic Press, 1995
Fenners, Pamela J. (ed)	*Waldorf Education a Family Guide* Michaelmas Press, 1999
Hemleben, Johannes	*Rudolf Steiner a Documentary Biography* Rudolph Steiner Press, 1975
Wachsmuth, Guenther	*The Life and Work of Rudolf Steiner: From the Turn of the Century to His Death* Gerber Communications, 1988

Index

Adyar (India), 50
agriculture, bio-dynamic, 155, 158
Akashic Record, 85–6
anabolic processes, 144
animal realm, 65–6
Anthroposophical Society, 98, 161
anthroposophy
    agriculture, 155, 158
    and artistic impulse, 99–102
    birth of, 58–9
    and Christianity, 96–8, 156–8
    education, 127–42
    eurythmy, 114–16
    evolution of the individual, 69–71, 78, 91–5
    Goethaenum, 102–14, 116, 120, 151, 159–60
    image of man, 66–9
    karma, 71, 72–5, 92, 130
    medicine, 143–54
    path of knowledge, 79–84
    'preamble' to, 53
    realms of nature, 64–5
    reincarnation, see reincarnation
    social organism, 120–6
    Steiner's legacy, 163–5
architecture, organic, 103–7
artistic eurythmy, 115
artistic expression, 99–102
astral body, 64–5, 66, 73, 91, 149
Atlantis, 86
auras, 76, 78

Bach, J. S., 30
Besant, Annie, 98
bio-dynamic agriculture, 155, 158
Blavatsky, Helena Petrovna, 50
Blie, Franziska, 6–7
Brockdorff, Count and Countess, 51
Bruno, Giordano, 74

Camphill movement (Scotland), 142
carpentry shop (at Goetheanum), 112, 115, 116, 160
catabolic processes, 144
Christianity
    and anthroposophy, 96–8, 156–8
    and 'image of man,' 66
    and reincarnation, 74
    Steiner's attitude to, 54
Chrysanthemum tea (1901), 57
clairvoyance, 17, 79
class conflict, 48
Collins, Mabel, 51
Community of Christians, 156
consciousness, stages of, 91
Copernicus, 2, 3
cosmology, 88–90, 97
Critique of Pure Reason, The (Kant), 13
cultural factors, 92, 93

Darwin, Charles, 14, 37, 88
disease, 147
Doctrine of Science (Fichte), 14
Dormach, Switzerland, 101
Drama Association, 45
drama mysteries, 100–2, 116

East-West Congress (1922), 157
education
    therapeutic, 141–2
    Waldorf schools, 127–40
educational eurythmy, 115
egoism, 125
equality, 123
Esoteric Buddhism (Sinett), 51
etheric body, 64–5, 66, 72, 73, 91, 149
Europe (post 1918), 122, 124
eurythmy, 114–16, 135, 136
    therapeutic, 115, 141, 154

evolution
  of the individual, 70–1, 78, 91–5
  of species, 37–8, 88
exercises, 79, 82
expressive art, 136
extra-sensory perception, 78

Faust (Goethe), 116
Fichte, Johann Gottlieb, 14, 74
formation of speech, 116
fraternity, 123
Free Literary Association, 44
freedom, 69, 73
  as goal of education, 130
French Revolution, 122, 123

Galileo, 2
genetics, 70, 92, 93
geometry, 11
German Lutheran church, 156
Goethe, Johann Wolfgang von
  Faust performance, 116
  metamorphosis of plants, ideas on 103
  and reincarnation, 74
  Schröer and, 22, 24
  Steiner's study of scientific work by, 23–5, 27, 29, 31, 53
Goethe and Schiller Archive, Weimar, 29
Goetheanum (at Dormach)
  construction of, 102–14
  Faust performed at, 116
  fire at, 159–60
  Higher School of Spiritual Sciences at, 120
  pharmaceutical production at, 151

Haeckel, Ernest, 35, 37–8
Hahn, H., 163
Hahnemann, Samuel, 153
healing process, 148–9
Hegel, Georg Wilhelm Friedrich, 14
Herder, Johann Gottfried, 30
Hess, Rudolf, 158

Hesse, Hermann, 124
Higher Independent School of Spiritual Science, The, 120
Hitler, Adolf, 140
homeopathy, 153
human aura, 76, 78
human individuality, 69–71, 78, 91–5
Hume, David, 74

'image of man,' 66–9
individuality, evolution of, 69–71, 78, 91–5
injustices of life, 94

Jesus Christ, 57, 97–8, 111

Kant, Immanuel, 13
karma, 71, 72–5, 92, 130
Krishnamurti, 98

labour movement, 46–7
Lessing, Doris, 74
liberty, 123; see also freedom
Light for the Way (Collins), 51
Lucifer (magazine), 60, 61, 62

Magazin für Literatur, 44–5, 48
materialism, 66, 70
meaning of life, 94
medicine, anthroposophical, 143–54
meditation, 40, 79
mental health, 83
metabolic-motor system, 144
mineral realm, 65–6
Molt, Emil, 127–8
moral sentiment, 93
Munich, Germany, 99–101
My Life Encounter with Rudolph Steiner (Rittelmeyer), 156

natural sciences, 39, 80
  and human individuality, 92

and perception, 78
neuro-sensory system, 143–4
Nietzsche, Friedrich Wilhelm, 35, 36, 51, 53

occult science, 62, 79, 80–3, 87
Olcott, Henry Steel, 50
organic architecture, 103–7

path of knowledge, 79–84, 120
Paul, Jean, 35
perception, 78, 149
pharmacopoeia, anthroposophical, 152–3
Philosophical-Theosophical Press, 62
phylogenesis, 37
physical body
   and consciousness, 91
   'packaging' of the, 64–5, 66
   and reincarnation, 72
Plato, 34
Poeppig, F., 163
progressive materialisation, 90
proletariat, 48, 125

realms of nature, 64–5
reincarnation
   and Christianity, 74
   and education, 130
   and human spirit, 71
   and Jesus of Nazareth, 97–8
   and sleep, 72–3
   and spiritual science, 92
   Steiner's approach to, 75
religious education, 138
'Representative of Humanity' (sculpture), 111
rhythmic system, 144
Richter, Johann Paul Friedrich (Jean Paul), 35
Rittelmeyer, Dr Friedrich, 156

scenic art, 116
Schelling, Friedrich, 14

Schiller, Friedrich, 30, 70
School for the Education of Workers (Berlin), 46–7
Schopenhauer, Arthur, 35, 74
Schröer, Karl Julius, 22, 24, 29
Schultz, Anna, 32
scientific knowledge, 21
scientific revolution, 2–3
self
   after death, 73
   and healing, 149
   and human individuality, 91–5
   as 'packaging' of physical body, 66
   and realms of nature, 64–5
   'Waldorf method' and, 130
self-healing, 150–4
self perpetuation, 94
Sinett, A. P., 51
Sivers, Marie von
   on building of Goetheanum, 102
   and devotion to Steiner's work, 59
   early life of, 55
   and eurythmy, 115
   and expressive art, 99, 100
   and *Lucifer* publication, 60
   marries Steiner, 117
   on outbreak of WW1, 108
   and Philosophical-Theosophical Press, 62
   and Steiner's lectures, 55, 119
   and Theosophical Society, 56–7
sleep, and reincarnation, 72
social organism, 123–6
special needs children, 141–2
spiritual eye, 76, 78, 79
   and path of knowledge, 79–84, 120
spiritual science, see anthroposophy
Steiner, Johann (father), 6–7, 15
Steiner, Rudolf
   and agriculture, 155
   and Anna Schultz, 32
   baptism of, 17
   birth and early life of, 7–9
   change in attitude of, 41
   and cosmology, 88–90, 97
   cultural circle of, 33
   distinct phases in work of, 59

and drama mysteries, 100–2
education of, 11–16
and evolution, 38–9
and fire at Goetheanum, 159–60
first experience of clairvoyance, 17
and Free Literary Association, 44
and Goethe, 22–5, 27, 29, 31, 53
illness and death of, 162
and karma, 73
lectures of, 118–19, 124, 145, 157–8
and Marie von Sivers, 55–7, 59, 60, 117
masters of, 18–20
and medicine, 143, 149–50
and meditation, 40
and Nietzsche, 35–6, 51, 53
parents of, 6–7
and positive attitude to other ideologies, 34–5
and reincarnation, 75
and social organism, 123–6
spiritual development of, 42–3
and system of education, 127–42
and Theosophy, 51–7, 61–3, 98
as tutor, 28
and Vienna cafés, 27
in Weimar, 29–41
works by
 Christianity as Mystical Fact, 53, 54
 Extending Practical Medicine, 146
 Friedrich Nietzsche: A Fighter for Freedom, 36, 51
 Haeckel and his Opponents, 38
 How to Know Higher Worlds, 62, 79, 80–3
 Metamorphoses of the Soul, 143
 Mysticism at the Dawn of the Modern Age, 53
 Outline of Occult Science, An, 62, 87
 Philosophy of Freedom, The, 39
 Theory of Knowledge Based on Goethe's World Conception, The 25, 27
 Theosophy (1904), 62, 63–5, 76, 79
 Towards Social Renewal, 124
supra-sensory organs, 66, 78, 87

teachers, 129–33
 and Waldorf method, 134
Theosophical Society
 aims of, 50
 German branch of, 56–7, 60
 and Messiah, 98
 Steiner's lecture tours for, 61
theosophy, 50
 and reincarnation, 74
 and Steiner's thinking, 52
therapeutic education, 141–2
therapeutic eurythmy, 115, 141, 154
Third Reich, 158
Turgenieff, A., 163

Uhland, Johann Ludwig, 35

vegetable realm, 65–6
veneration, 138
vital force, 86

Wagner, Richard, 74
Waldorf schools, 127–40
water, image of, 68
Wegman, Ita, 145–6
Weimar, Germany, 29–41
Weleda company, 151
Wheeler, Montague, 106
Wieland, Christoph Martin, 30, 35
working classes, 48, 125
World War I, 108–9, 113, 122
World's Trade Fair, 1

Zeylmans van Emmichoven, F. W., 163

The Authors

Lía Tummer works as a German and English translator. Her first contact with anthroposophy came with studying in Waldorf schools. Through reading and translating anthroposophical texts, she has become an expert in all its fields.

Lato (Horacio Santana) is an Argentinian cartoonist. He has illustrated stories for *Dartagnan*, *El Tony*, *Fantasía* and other popular magazines.